June 18, 1998

AYMOND

For Benno, a young Egyptian
from an old Egyptian + with
many thanks for much help
through the years

Very Fondly

AYMOND

A Novel by A. G. Burkhart, Jr.

SUNSTONE
PRESS

SANTA FE
New Mexico

The events, people, and incidents in this story are the sole product of the author's imagination. The story is fictional and any resemblance to individuals living or dead is purely coincidental.

Sunstone books may be purchased for edcational, business, or sales promotional use. For information please write: Special Markets Department, Sunstone Press, P.O. Box 2321, Santa Fe, New Mexico 87504-2321.

FIRST EDITION

10 9 8 7 6 5 4 3 2 1

Library of Congress Cataloging in Publication Data:
Burkhart, A.G., 1925-
    Aymond: a novel / by A.G. Burkhart. —1st ed.
      p. cm.
    ISBN: 0-86534-258-X
    I. Title.
PS3552.U7246A9   1997
813'.54—dc21   96-45294
                CIP

Published by   SUNSTONE PRESS
                Post Office Box 2321
                Santa Fe, NM 87504-2321 / USA
                (505) 988-4418 / orders only (800) 243-5644
                FAX (505) 988-1025

TO THE INTRACTABLE TARA

With warm thanks to Martha Briggs
for reading my electroscript and for encouragement

And to
Wanda Little, for generous proofing, corrections,
suggestions, and further encouragement

And to
James Clois Smith, Jr. and Ralph Schwab
for erudite corrections and removal of verbosity

And to
Mary Jane Vinzant for final proofing.

CHAPTER 1

THE SNOW WHISPERED AROUND the hooves of Jericho, a hustling palomino, being pushed rapidly on by a nineteen year old with hair the same golden color as his steed. Aymond had broad shoulders and a very trim waist, though he had not yet filled out as much as he would. A fleece lined coat was pulled tight against the biting cold. The icy northern wind was bitter coming off the plains and snow swirled around him. It was beginning to fill the tracks he was following and the thought of losing the trail pushed him harder. There were two horses ahead, both well shod and moving easily.

He had read the signs carefully at the burnt wagon now miles behind him. The man had been slowly killed while tied to the rear wheel, his arms pushed between the spokes and tied beneath the axle. The fire had taken some of his flesh off but not enough to hide the hideous cuts and mangling. His private parts had been cut off and shoved in his mouth. The scalp was gone but Aymond had found it tossed under a nearby blackberry bush. The woman had been killed by a hatchet wound to the lower abdomen and allowed to bleed to death as a large brown stain around her indicated. Her face was dark, contorted in death. Aymond had ached, sensing the torment she must have undergone. What had troubled him even more were the foot prints of two small children. He searched and found no bodies or hints of burials. He knew there would have been no burials but he wanted to be certain. The only other thing was another horse which had bled to death from a bullet wound in the neck.

The villain had tried to make his work look like that of Indians but an occasional missed boot heel mark betrayed the perpetrator.

He had tried carefully to remove all signs but Aymond's keen eyes had spotted them. They were totally unlike the farm brogans worn by the murdered settler or the high laced shoes of his wife. Farther out, Aymond had been able to see where the murderer must have lifted the two children onto one horse and then mounted the other. Aymond had wondered why the bastard was taking along the two children except possibly as hostages. Aymond Bearman, though only nineteen, was a man grown. He had done man's work since age twelve, had been on two cattle drives to Kansas and had survived a shoot-out in Dodge City where one of the hard cases had fallen to his Winchester. He was not unused to the hard choices and conditions of the open prairies. This outrage near the west Texas staked plains, he felt, left him no choice but to follow the trail of the kidnapped children and take them from the bastard. He even relished the idea of giving that hard case a little of his own. He frowned. Notions like this would have to be fought or he would turn into the same sort of creature. Even though Aymond's past would have allowed it, his later training was adverse to such cruel behavior.

First he had struggled to dig a grave. He carried no shovel and the handle of the one that had been on the wagon had been consumed in the fire. The metal was still there, a sure indication it was not the work of Indians who passed up no chance to acquire additional iron or steel. They had learned to work it but most were incapable of smelting it from ore. After a few minutes of digging, he found his skillet worked better. Upon getting them in the ground he salvaged a partially burned board and wrote the date 1875 and KILLED BY A WHITE SKINNED SKUNK. He wanted to be sure no one blamed it on Indians.

He had started after the two horses, deciding that there was no real hurry for him to get to Lizard Sands where his mentor, Doc Bearman, was mending the local lame. By then he estimated that the threesome had about a three day margin ahead of him.

The tracks had started off north, the direction from which Aymond had been coming. He had been heading south toward Lizard Sands and was halfway between Kiowa and Commanche territory. In fact, they overlapped in this area, which made it necessary to keep a full look-out for hunting and war parties. February was ready to turn into March and the first signs of spring had started to appear with swellings on the willows and a few early buds. This meant the wintering tribes were beginning to stir and resuming activity, especially hunting to replenish diminished larders. After being shut up they could be doubly vicious. Double vigilance was the answer even though he was sure they would stay in their wickiups until the blizzard blew over, but they could have been caught out and so caution was never a mistake. Constantly watching his backtrail and consistently following the horizon with his eyes was second nature to him. Now was not the time to try to palaver with storm irked Comanches.

— — —

Ay knew all about the Comanche tribe that had killed his parents when he was five and then had taken him into the group where he had learned to survive in the wilderness, to make small bows and arrows, how to shoot a musket, and naturally to speak the language with the best of them. He had then been snatched up by Apaches when he was eight and carried off to the mountains where he stayed until he was twelve, learning Apache ways and lingo along with a little Spanish. He had been well instructed in tracking and surviving in difficult places until he had been trussed up howling and flailing in 1868 by a calvary troop that had recognized him as white while raiding his village. A calvary stallion's heavy hoof had smashed the spralled boy's right ankle.

The only thing the platoon's Navajo scout had gotten out of him was that his name was Three Trees. This was the name given him by the kindly Commanche woman who had taken him in hand. He had conveyed this information by sign language to the Apaches who continued to use the same name.

The troop had stopped at Lizard Sands to have the wounded tended by Doc Bearman who took an immediate interest in the white boy he treated for a crushed foot. Ay could still catch a few English words and as the days passed began to use it again in a halting way. He answered to Three Trees in English.

9

Doc finally sat him down after he had been in Lizard Sands a few months and tried to pick his memory. Three Trees could remember coming across the prairie in a wagon with a white top. He had a dim memory of his folks being killed and of being taken to a Comanche village and handled by Soft Wind, an old squaw with no husband. She had cuddled him and crooned Indian lullabies. He had gathered wood for her and had quckly learned the ways of spotting animal and human tracks and making use of the knowledge. With that ability he early on was able to shoot and trap rabbits, turkeys, raccoons and other wild game. He was taught to make his own small bow with fire hardened arrows feathered from crow wings. The tribe had provided buffalo and horse meat which Soft Wind cut into small strips and dried. The other boys taught him to ride and play games on horseback. As his skin darkened under the Texas sun, he had found complete acceptance by his playmates and even found a girl, Swift Deer, a year younger, who seemed fond of him. They often swam together and played chasing and hiding games. It had been a happy time with the Comanches.

Naturally he had been sad for a while after Hawk Scream, the Apache warrior, caught him during a raid, but with his young nature he had easily adapted to the new life. Hawk Scream had turned him over to his squaw, Green Willow, who took him to heart as had Soft Wind. Green Willow was pleased to have a son. She had two grown daughters whose braves were not known as good providers. They loved the white man's fire water and would rather remain soused than hunt or join raiding parties. Old Hawk Scream took the boy in hand and showed him many examples of Indian wiles.

Three Trees learned to conceal himself in a two-inch depression with five inches of grass; how to stay downwind when stealing horses and was lucky enough to be presented with a real Bowie knife Hawk Scream had taken from a downed trooper. Even when grown, Three Trees still kept this knife that Hawk Scream had so carefully taught him how to use in a feral fight with feints and slashes and how to keep the edge razor sharp. Three Trees slowly became an adept fighter but was not so easily accepted by the youngsters of the new group who looked on him as an outsider. But, as he rapidly learned the speech and joined in the activities, they grew cooperative and began to show him the Apache ways. In turn he showed them a few Comanche tricks and they grew friendlier.

After four years with the tribe, Three Trees felt like a full fledged Apache when the soldiers came. His foot had been shattered by a horse as he fell while running for the woods and then snatched up by the trooper. Continually he fought against his captivity and resolved to get away as soon as he could, but his foot was slow healing.

Doc Bearman had to set and reset the bones, each time utilizing a formidable plaster cast, but he constantly assured Three Trees it was going to heal, but as the foot improved Doc realized Three Trees would always have a slight limp. Three Trees had hated the heavy weight on his lower leg and at first had tried to remove it. Doc Bearman, with the help of a transient Navajo, explained what was happening. As Three Trees settled down to await his healing, he became adept in English. After all it was his mother tongue. It came back easily and his vocabulary grew rapidly.

With the help of Mary Jane O'Kelly, Doc's girl friend, and his black family, Mandy and Diogenes, Three Trees was taught to read and started on a course of arithmetic, history, and writing. He remained sharp and, as in the past, learned rapidly.

One evening, Doc showed Three Trees a book by Dickens called *A Tale of Two Cities.* "You'll enjoy this I think. It will help you with words and give you a little history. Sit down a minute, I want to ask you a few things.

"I know you barely remember your mother and father but do your remember what their names were? What did they call each other?"

"Well...Mother called him father and father called her mother. That's what I called them." He squirmed as his puckered face indicated unease in not knowing.

"No other names for each other that you can remember?" Doc was adamant.

"No sir."

"Sure about that? Stop and think."

"No sir. That's it."

"Then what did they call you?"

Three Trees stopped and thought. "It was Aymond."

"Aymond, Aymond, that's a funny name. Are you sure that's right?"

"Yes. It was Aymond."

"Could it have been Amos?"

"No. It was Aymond."

Actually, he had been christened Raymond but, while barely able to talk, insisted on calling himself Aymond and his parents had laughingly fallen in with the childishness, feeling it would be easily straightened out when he was older.

But it was never straightened out. Aymond could never remember a family name either.

Aymond was given Doc's last name of Bearman. Although he never adopted him, Doc made Aymond feel like a member of the family and seemed to prefer him over the other orphans and foundlings that Doc was constantly gathering around him while he found them a home. Doc had wanted to adopt Aymond but quickly realized this was not allowed for bachelors. He could not get Mary Jane O'Kelly to marry him though he kept trying. They were good friends and buddies, maybe even in love, but she felt she would encase him in bad luck with matrimony. She had lost three husbands before she was thirty. So Doc remained a widower and Mary Jane remained a very close friend and helped out with the youngsters and became something of a mother figure for them.

When seventeen, Ay had been sent to the University of Virginia by Doc who felt that time at his old Alma Mater would improve him. It did. He had even learned to box in the eastern or British manner. He met Doc's brother, Joseph Bearman, near Thoroughfare Gap in Virginia and received a Southerner's view of The War Between the States. Doc did not talk about it much, though he had amputated many a limb and stopped infections in both Rebels and Yanks while serving with Lee's army of Northern Virginia.

Joseph became very taken with the boy and insisted on giving him a three year old palomino which was a strange mixture of Arabian, Morgan, Thoroughbred, and a little bit of western mustang from a gift stallion that Doc has sent his brother by boat at the time Aymond left for college. The Arabian strain had resulted in a rich creamy coat of the lightest tan. Joe laughed that it almost matched Ay's hair. Joe had even made the arrangements for the horse to travel the same train to Kansas City so Aymond would have him for the trek home. Remembering stories that Diogenes had told him in his youth of the golden air around Jericho before Joshua blew his horn, Ay decided Jericho would be a good name because the city had lasted even after its walls had come tumbling down. Jericho just sounded like a grand name for a grand horse even though he was young.

Aymond decided to stop his college work for a while and try his hand at ranching. Doc agreed. Ay had visions of becoming a medical doctor too and the elder Bearman had encouraged him, even promising to fund his stay at Edinburgh to gurantee him the very best of medical training. Doc had studied there and since that time its reputation had continued to grow. Medicine was becoming more of a science every day and the advances in techniques were breath-taking. Doc had continued to receive the journals associated with the school although they were slow in coming and much behind date by the time he got them but were still revelations of exciting new things. Doc passed this excitement on to Aymond who had done preliminary work at Virginia, studying chemistry and physics as well as continuing his work in the necessary Latin and then, for fun, Greek, with an overview of English language and history. Aymond, as well as Doc, felt he was well prepared for medical school by the end of his second year but Aymond had convinced his father, as so he looked upon him, to let him take a year or two off from his studies to satisfy his wanderlust and to be sure he was suited to being a physician. This had met with Doc's approval and Aymond headed home to decide on his next move. He had caught the train to Kansas City and was proceeding by his gratuitous mount to Lizard Sands when he had run into the ambuscade of the little wagon train in Comanche territory.

— — —

13

Yes, Aymond Bearman knew Comanches. He kept an eye out for them as he followed the trail north for about three miles where it disappeared among some rocks. Ay felt that the man had not continued north since he had seen no trace of him coming down. Since Cain (as Ay had now christened him in his mind) had approached the wagon from the east, it would seem he would continue to the west. A long swing to the west confirmed this. The trail was not hard to spot or follow. The man apparently knew very little about tracking or hiding trails. Other than the first move to travel north and hide his hoof prints among the rocks he had shown no ingenuity. Ay followed easily and rapidly. He came across the camp where they had spent the first night. A quick examination of the site showed that the older and heavier child had apparently been tied up. He had even hopped to relieve himself. From foot size and water remains Ay had satisfied himself it was a boy about the age of eight to ten. The other child was a girl of about four or five. She had been allowed to move freely. There was no indication of mistreatment of the children while the second day's camp indicated they were being fed and cared for.

CHAPTER 2

AYMOND WAS CATCHING UP, BEING now no more than a day and a half behind them. It was then that the weather started turning cold and clouds came in from the southwest. He thought by the way the clouds were moving that there would be a spring cloud-burst but the temperature continued to drop and the swirling winds brought snow. He pushed on more rapidly and did not stop when he came onto another night's camp. He could see at a glance the rabbit bones and knew that Cain hunted while moving along. Earlier track activity had foretold it and he was pleased to have his speculations confirmed.

He pushed on, hoping to catch up before the tracks were covered.

Late in the afternoon when the dark of twilight had arrived early he came from behind a tree at the top of a knoll, being careful not to show against the skyline, and spotted a log cabin with no signs of life. A wagon stood in front of a small barn and the smaller cabin had no smoke showing. A rough corral stood empty with several rails down. He stopped about a hundred yards away and yelled, "Ahoy the cabin." There was no answer. He approached to about fifty yards and repeated the call. Still no answer. As he approached he sighted a figure slumped against the back wheel of the wagon.

"Oh no!" Ay cried aloud. As he got closer he heard groaning. Quickly dismounting, he grabbed his Winchester and immediately checked the interior of the barn. No dangers there. A glance at the figure told Ay it was a boy about thirteen or fourteen. Without stopping, he ran in a zig-zag way to the cabin, dropped to his knees and looked in the open door. Again nothing. He returned to the boy whose face was a bloody pulp. The moaning continued. He was obviously much alive, although very battered. Ay crawled under the wagon and loosened the raw hide. It was necessary to cut it in only one spot as it had not shrunk much from the moisture of the snow. The boy tumbled forward on his face and made burbling sounds. Ay quickly backed out and turned him over. The boy had passed out, so he gathered him up and took him inside the cabin. As he turned to shut the door he noticed another body, stark naked, stretched out behind the trough. It was a middle aged woman. Ay groaned this time. He knew what it meant.

Removing his flint and steel and with some shavings and bark from a nearby box. he started a fire. He put down a blanket and placed the boy on it, covering him with another, and then walked out of the cabin to the trough.

The woman had been long dead and was cold and hard to the touch. He went back in the cabin and grabbed a blanket from the other bunk, returned to the woman and spread it over her. He then walked down to his horse.

The palomino had been standing patiently in the snow and cold. Ay placed his Winchester against a post out of the snow, loosened the top strap of his holster and checked his converted Colt. It was in good shape and the cylinder turned easily. He slid it back into the holster and turned to the horse, removed the saddle, took it inside the barn and tossed it over a stable gate. Taking the horse inside he undid the bridle and took off the saddle bags and blanket, then rubbing the gelding down with hay. After finding some dry corn in a rack, he scooped some up and put it in a wood feeding tray. The horse munched hungrily while Aymond found a fork and put more hay into the stall.

Satisfied now that Old Gold was properly cared for, he went outside and started looking for signs of what had happened. He immediately found the tracks of three horses heading away west. He guessed Cain had picked up a pack horse from the corral and was continuing his trek better prepared. He started back for the cabin, paused, and looked at the blanket covered figure, and then opened the door. The boy was quiet under the blanket and the fire was about

out. Ay added a couple of sticks from the wood box and then put on a split bit of wood from along side it. In a few minutes it was flaming nicely again.

Cans and canisters had been turned over and contents spilled. Sacks and cases had been cut open with contents missing. A small mound of coffee was spilled on the floor, and Ay gathered it up and put it in a tin. He found a coffee pot upside down in a corner with a crushed side evidencing a hard kick. He pushed it back out as well as he could and filled it from a bucket hanging by the fireplace. He ladled in some of the dirty coffee and put it on a rack in the fireplace. He then turned back to the boy who was stirring some.

Ay moistened a cloth in the bucket and wiped the lad's face. The nose was broken and pushed to one side. Ay had often watched Doc Bearman straighten busted noses and he, with no hesitation, grabbed the appendage and pulled. Something popped and the boy yelled and started flailing his arms. Ay held him and made crooning noises until he became still. The nose looked straight and much better. Ay felt certain that the boy would not be fooling with it even if it hurt and so made no effort to bandage it. He was not even sure he could do it and still allow for breathing.

The pain had wakened the youngster and he was looking wildly around him. Ay continued the crooning melodies and then whispered. "Everything's all right now. Just relax, you're not going to be hurt any more. Your nose was busted and I straightened it out so it would heal right. You're going to be fine," Ay said assuringly.

The boy relaxed and then started whimpering. Ay continued to hold him. "Everything's all right. Yes, all right. You're not going to be hurt any more. My name is Aymond and I was riding by and found you tied to the wagon. I got you loose and brought you in here. Everything is going to be fine now."

"Where's Ma? What's he done to Ma?" the boy cried more than asked.

"There's nothing you can do now. You've got to rest and get your strength back. Now let's get you on your bunk so you can get better."

"What's happened to Ma? Where's my Ma? I gotta know!" the boy insisted.

Ay figured he might just as well have it affirmed now since he had a good idea the boy had seen his mother killed. "She's dead, son." Ay felt strange calling him son when the boy was almost as old as he. "Yes, he finished her off. We'll have to get her buried."

Tears came to the boy's eyes and he cried softly for a while and stopped. "Cryin' won't do no good. I've got to git him, I'll goin' to git dat murderin' skunk!"

Ay started slightly when he realized the boy had called Cain the same thing he had put on the grave marker. "And I prided myself on having a good vocabulary. It shows how limited I am," he thought. "That kid has labeled him just like me and I've a sneaking feeling he hasn't read anything except the Bible if even that."

"What's your name young man? We're going to be working together and I'll need to know. Like I told you my name's Aymond Bearman but a lot of folks call me Ay."

"I'm George, Ay. George Allen. My Ma was Elizabeth Allen or Mrs. Henry Allen. Dad was killed by Kiowas about two years ago. Oh Ma! Oh Ma!" George began crying quietly again.

Aymond put his arm around the boy's shoulders and knew he had to get his attention away from his sorrows. "We'll need to straighten up around here and get you mother buried. Now you tell me where your shovel is and then stretch out so you can get your strength back. You can't go chasing a killer when you're half out."

"Dere's a shovel in the barn. Oh Ma."

"I'll get it. Now you hop in that bunk." Ay watched George drag himself over and crawl in. He then started briskly for the barn.

The snow had slowed down and showed signs of stopping with true darkness fast coming on but not enough to hide a small cross on a nearby knoll which Ay guessed had to be Henry Allen. He walked over and carved into the wood was: "Henry Allen 1833-1872 RIP."

Ay walked on to the barn and found an ax and shovel in the tool bin. He walked back to the knoll and next to Henry's grave started loosening the earth with the ax. He hated to take a good edge off a useful tool but he could see this ax had been abused. He would chop the earth with it and then grind it to sharpness some other time. He got the earth loose and then switched to the shovel. Working steadily he had removed enough dirt in about an hour and a half. The movement had kept him warm though the wind was colder. He took off his gloves and went back to the cabin where George was now asleep. Aymond put more wood on the fire and waited for it to blaze up. He noticed the coffee pot and thought, "Man I need that." He poured a his cup full, thick with grounds, and located the sugar canister on the floor against the back wall. He added three big spoonfuls to his beverage and sipped on the scorching drink. It revived him.

While looking around and behind a curtain, he found a niche with a few clothes hanging. He took what was probably Elizabeth's best dress from the tiny selection and went outside. He started to take the body inside, thought better of it and left it where it was. His Bowie knife neatly split the dress up the back, Elizabeth, as he was beginning to think of her, was frozen quite stiff from the cold as well as death. His heart sank as he thought of the wickedness of Cain who had destroyed the essence of the lives of two families. He would need punishment and stopping.

Aymond removed the blanket and propped her upright against the trough. He pushed the dress on from the front, turned her around and fastened it with a couple of pins in the back. He put her back down and recovered her with the blanket.

Back in the cabin, with the idea of waking George and finishing with the burial bit, he found George was still sleeping peacefully and decided to leave him be and have the burial in the morning. Besides he was right tired. Thinking that he had been trailing since morning, had dug a grave, and now had an invalid on his hands, the full realization dawned on him that on top of every thing else, he was ravishingly hungry. "Enough to eat a raw cow," he thought. The remembrance of some cans on the floor in the clothes niche led to five cans of peaches, two of which he quietly opened and finished off in a hurry, He sweetened some more hot coffee and began to feel better.

Ay took his Winchester and placed it next to the head of the other bunk, removed his gun belt and hung it from a peg by the bunk, took out the Colt and placed it under the blanket about half way down and sat down on the bunk, removed his boots and sighed in satisfaction. He got up and rechecked the door being certain that the latch was thrown and the bar down and the ones over the shutters of the four windows were tight. Then stretching out on the bunk with his clothes on, then pulling up the blanket, he was immediately asleep.

— — —

Aymond awoke before dawn with a full bladder screaming for attention. His internal alarm clock awakened him instinctively. This time both methods cooperated. His bladder could wait a few minutes while he went to each window to check the surrounding countryside in the first glolight of the morning. Seeing nothing amiss and no tracks other than his own in the snow he returned to the bunk, sat down, reached over and picked up both boots. He pounded them up side down against his open palm to be sure no night creatures had crawled in for warmth and then eased them on. While outside, Aymond also found Jericho in good shape.

George was still sleeping quietly and soundly. Ay cut some bacon from a cured side hanging from a rafter. He put the Allen's big skillet in the fireplace and restarted the fire. George stirred at the sound of the steel and flint. Ay located some scorched biscuits in the Dutch oven and put them in the skillet to warm in the bacon drippings. Ay loved biscuits cooked in bacon fat and could eat them forever.

The smell and movement finally awakened George. The youngster sat up, stretched and yawned. His eyes fell on Ay tending the skillet and the awful reality of yesterday dawned on him. He gave a half cry and Ay turned quickly reaching for his pistol. He relaxed as he saw no problem.

"Breakfast will be ready in a few minutes. Do you think you can stir around some?"

"I guess," came hesitantly from George.

"Try washing your face but be easy around your nose. It's broken. Try to get on some clean clothes while I finish up here. Don't push yourself. If you can't cut it, just stretch back out. It's all right— no rush."

20

Ay scooped up more of the retrieved coffee, added it to the pot, then ladled water into it from the bucket. The boy was moving slowly but washed off his face and went outside. He came back in, went to the clothes niche and came back with a change of Levis and a woolen shirt. He slowly squirmed into another set of long johns after stripping off the bloody ones. With the clean pants and shirt he looked totally new. His face was still raw but the clothing hid most of the other problems.

"I think I've gotta broken rib where he kicked me but I kin git around," the boy said softly.

"Find a long piece of cloth or a sheet or we can even cut up one of your mother's old dresses into strips and I'll bind it for you after breakfast."

George pulled back the curtain again, looked at his mother's dresses and started crying quietly. The whole of the tragedy was engulfing him. Aymond walked over and put his arm around the boy's shoulder, standing quietly and saying nothing. George straightened up and said, "Thanks."

"Nothing," answered Ay. "Come on and have some breakfast."

George gobbled down the biscuits, not realizing these were the last he would ever have cooked by his mother. The bacon was quick to follow. Ay was pleased to see the healthy appetite. It meant the boy was not hurt bad and would recover soon.

"Have some of this coffee. It's strong and will perk you up." George took a cup and put in five spoons of sugar. "Really like yours sweet, don't you?"

"Only way I can git it down. You make it like Ma does... did." Tears formed again, as his voice stopped.

"Well, we've got to get your mother buried. I've fixed a spot next to your Dad, so put on something warm and come outside if you can make it."

"I kin make it," he insisted as he squirmed into an overly large wool jacket. Obviously it had been his father's.

George followed Ay outside. "I've gotta see'r agin." He stooped and drew back the blanket. "Oh Ma." He saw that she had on her best dress. "Oh Ma," the lad cried. He stared hard and long at her face. "I'm all right now. Let's go," as he replaced the blanket around her corpse.

The two carried the small bundle up the hill toward the grave site. Ay could see that it was a strain for the boy in his present condition and stopped halfway. "Let's rest a minute." George sat quietly and then after a few minutes they finished the trek.

"I've gotta see'r agin," George insisted. He unwrapped his mother's face and cried softly, "Oh Ma." It was barely audible. He remained some time and then "I'm ready," as he recovered her face. The snow had continued during the night and the bottom of the grave was covered with snow. "She'll have soft snow to rest on," as they lowered her in.

"Why don't you go get your Bible and I'll read John three-sixteen for her." The boy struggled down to the cabin and returned with the well-worn book. Ay had felt the moments alone were what George needed. The Bible was not necessary, he knew the verse by heart but felt it more appropriate to read it.

He opened the Bible, found the verse and recited, "'For God so loved the world that He gave his only begotten son that whosoever believeth in Him should not perish but have everlasting life.'" He paused, "Why don't you go back and stretch out for a while and I'll finish up here." George quietly obeyed.

Aymond filled the grave and piled stones on top to keep out animals. He went to the barn and found two boards and nails and formed a crude cross and returned to the cabin. After blowing on his hands to warm them, he pulled out his Bowie knife, pushed back a chair, sat with the cross resting on the table and started carving Elizabeth Allen.

"When was your mother born?"

"I think it was 1839. She jist turned 36. That's right 1839."

Aymond cut 1839-1875 underneath the name on the crossbar. "This is ready now. Do you feel up to going back while we put it in?" The boy climbed from the bunk. "Let's go."

Ay tapped the cross into the hard ground, put his arm around George and slowly helped him back to the cabin while saying, "I'm going to have to take off after that bastard now so he won't get away."

"I'll go too. I'll git'm and make him pay for what he done to my Ma. I'll git'm; I'll git'm; I will! You'll see."

"There's no way. There's only the one horse and you'll slow me down if I ride you and you're in no condition to travel anyway, especially in this cold."

"But I gotta go. He come in sayin' he needed a spot to shelter them two kids for the night and Ma fixed them a good meal. After he finished he said he'd show me his pistol and hit me in the face. He beat me up some more and tied me up and made me watch what he done to Ma. Sumphun musta scared him off 'fore he finished me, but I'm agoin' to git'm if it's the last thing I do. I'm goin' to kill'm slow."

"Whoa, now. Whoa. You're in no shape to be chasing a mean coyote like that. He'd only do you in again and you might not last this time. Get your strength back first. I'll take care of him and if I can't, I'll come back here for you. How's that?"

"No way. I'm goin'," George insisted.

"Use your head, son, You're holding me up and you know you can't keep up. Stay here so I can find you later."

"I ain't promisin' nuddin."

"Think it over. How about scrounging up some grub for me to take while I'm saddling my horse. I'll need to get moving so I won't lose the trail."

"All right," came from George grudgingly.

After Aymond had stuffed his saddle bags with the food and cans, he inquired, "What's the next place over west of here?"

"That's the Matlocks. The ole man and two grown boys with his wife and three girls. Nah, he won't try nuddin on them."

"How far is it?"

"I reckon about thirty miles. You kin do it in a day easy if you moves along." Ay started off, then stopped and turned his horse.

"Oh yea, what did your horse look like?"

"He was mostly black with three white stockings."

"And the man?"

"About average height. A belly comin' up. Very black hair, cut short, needed a shave. Black hat with a small brim, brown wool

23

shirt, red bandanna around his neck, long black coat and cowboy boots. Kinda a mixture. His eyes were dark brown, almost black."

"You sure saw a good deal."

"The bastard, and ya sho gave'm the right name, saw to it I had the time and he'll always be inma mem'ry lika picture.

"Well, I'm gone. Now you stay here, get well, and wait for me."

"Ain't promisin' nuddin," the boy reiterated.

"If you're better before I get back and feel like moving you better go on over to Lizard Sands. That's where my home is. It's west and south of here."

"I've heard of it."

"My father's Doc Bearman and he'll put you up until you and I can get together. He's a good man and he'll watch out for you. Main thing is for you to get better before you move out of here. Go to the Matlocks first. Then go on in easy stages if you need to. Tell Dad I sent you if I'm not there or haven't been there. If I haven't caught him by the time I check in at Lizard Sands we'll trail together after him."

"Yeh, that'l work and thanks. I really mean it, Thanks,"

"Don't mention it, kid. Be sure you wait for me at Lizard Sands if I don't make it back here."

Aymond turned Jericho and headed west.

CHAPTER 3

AROUND MID-AFTERNOON AYMOND could make out a column of smoke from behind the next hill. Meanwhile there were many traces of Cain: broken branches, hoof prints in sheltered spots and tramped areas where stops had been made. Ay had pushed Jericho until the horse showed signs of severe fatigue. He eased him up the hill while staying within a clump of trees. The glen was much like the Allen one except the cabin was larger. Smoke rose from the chimney and about a dozen horses were in the corral. He did not see a black with three white stockings. Cattle were standing in the distance.

He approached slowly and yelled, "Hello, the cabin," and waited until shortly afterwards a muscular, middle aged man with a rifle cradled stepped out the door-way.

"What's it about, stranger?" he called.

"I just need to talk to you a minute."

"Come on up easy. There's plenty of help here so don't try anything." A hulking young man pressed his way out the door and looked over his father's shoulder.

Aymond kept his hands in sight and rode up part way, dismounted and led his horse up to the man with the rifle. "You must be Mr. Matlock."

"Yeah, that's me, John Matlock. What did you want?"

"I'm trying to catch up with a man and two kids. He must have come this way."

"Yeah, he left out of here this morning. Left for Haley's Crossing. What's the problem?"

"My horse is all shagged out. Do you mind if I give him a rest, maybe a quick rub down and a feed? It's been right cold out and he's in bad need of attention."

"Go ahead. Always 'mired a man who takes care of his horseflesh. When you finish come in for some hot coffee and vittles."

"Thanks much." Ay led his horse into the barn, unsaddled him and started rubbing him down with hay. He found some oats in a nearby bin and fed him. Leaving him munching at the feed bag, Ay headed for the cabin.

The whole family was gathered. The muscular old man and the two husky sons and two girls of about nineteen and seventeen stood back by the hearth watching him. An older woman with her back to him was stirring a pot while a young girl of about ten was hanging on to her mother's skirt and looking back over her shoulder at Ay. The cabin had rooms opening off the central one. This large family obviously needed the space.

Ay walked up to Mr. Matlock, stuck out his hand and shook. "Mr. Matlock, I'm Aymond Bearman. Sure kind of you folks to take me in."

"This here's my wife, Big Jenny, Mrs. Matlock, Little Jenny," indicating the nineteen year old, "Mary," the seventeen year old, "and little Helen, the baby of the family and Tucker, my oldest and John, Junior. I thinks that takes care of everybody. Now sit down and big Jenny'll have the fixings on in jist a minute. Little Helen, bring our guest a cup of that hot coffee."

Helen, a small ten year old, went to the fireplace where a large kettle hung from a bracket. She picked up a padded pot holder and pulled the swinging bracket from over the flame, lifted off the kettle, picked up a cup from the sideboard, put it front of Ay and poured the coffee. She then quietly returned the kettle to its bracket and shoved it over the fire.

With the coffee was in hand, Ay looked at Helen and grinned, "Thank you, Miss Helen." The girl grinned back shyly as he took a large pull and felt the warmth swelling out to his frozen limbs. It was good to have the radiance from the fireplace thawing his outside. He rubbed his arms and legs, looked up and grinned again. "This sure beats that ice house outside."

He noticed the two older girls looking at him sideways and giggling softly. He thought they were the prettiest pair of fillies he had seen in the west and far outshone many of the young ladies he had known back east. They were almost a matched pair. He would certainly like to know them better when there was time. The nineteen year old had maybe a slight edge over her sister, he thought.

Mrs. Matlock served beef stew in the bowls scattered around the table, adding an extra portion to Ay's bowl. Everyone waited as she returned the iron pot to the fireplace and took her seat next to her husband. All heads bowed as he said, "For what we are about to receive, makes us truly thankful, Oh Lord. Amen." And the race was on as all of them fed like there was no tomorrow. The stew vanished quickly while Ay tried to keep up and found with his intense hunger that it went down well.

"Now young man, what's this about Mr. Arnold and his kids?"

"Is that the name he gave you? Well, they're not his kids and I'm out to catch him and take them away from him."

"What are you talking about?" Matlock asked. "Those were very nice kids and Mr. Arnold was a very fine gentleman. The kids were quiet and well behaved, not at all noisy and cutting up like mine did." He looked around the table and faces turned sideways or down.

"Well, they're not his. He held up some wagoneers east of here and killed everybody and ran off with the kids. I figure he's using them for hostages or bait. It was horrible how he kills women. I can't even tell you about it, it was so bad."

"I can't believe this about Mr. Arnold. What about you Jenny? Does this sound right to you?

"No, John. He seemed like such a nice man and the children minded so well."

"They were probably scared to death. I've got to get that man," Ay injected.

"Just a minute, let me check something," said Mr. Matlock rising. He went into the other room, returned and stood behind Bearman. He poked a large pistol into the back of Ay's neck, pulled back the hammer and said, "Now stand up real slow young man and don't try anything. John Junior get his gun!"

"Hey, what's happening?" Ay insisted.

"Shut up and sit back down. Tucker, get some rope and tie him to that chair. You just sit still my fine Mr. Bearman. Going to do in good citizens with nice kids, are you? Well, we'll see. Put your hands through those spokes behind you. Tie him good, Tucker. We don't want a varmint like this gettin' loose."

"What's going on here? I haven't done anything. What's wrong with y'all?"

"We know your kind. Cause trouble for everybody. Is he tached up good Tucker?"

"Yes sir. No way he's goin' to get loose."

"Will you please sit down and let me explain."

"No way you're going to talk your way out of this. You just sit there and be quiet while I figure out what to do with you."

"But you're wrong and I can explain it so you'll understand."

"Keep quiet now or we'll put a gag on you."

"Ah, Daddy," injected little Jenny, "it's not going to hurt to let him say something. He looks like a nice young man anyway."

"Yeah, he's a fine young man! Now little Jenny, you stay out of this. This is men's business and we don't want you young girls gittin' involved and messin' things up."

"Ah, Mama, get Daddy to let him talk."

"I don't know Little Jenny; your father's a pretty smart man and he's always taken care of us."

"But talking never hurts anything. Let him talk!"

"Well maybe she's right John," big Jenny conceded. "Let's just hear what he's got to say. After all he is tied up."

"All right, but I'm not really likin' it. Go ahead and spread your lies."

"They aren't lies, Mr. Matlock. Tell me, did this Arnold have a black horse with him with three white stockings?

"Yes, he did that."

"Have you ever seen that horse before?"

"Well, the Allens had one similar."

"Well, I'm going to tell you that skunk Arnold killed Mrs. Allen and I buried her this morning. The boy, George, was beaten pretty bad and couldn't come because that bastard took their horse."

"I kinda thought that was the Allen horse, Dad, but I didn't want to say nothin'."

"That so, Tucker? What about you Junior? You've seen that horse."

"I was sure it was the Allen horse, Pa, but I didn't think it was polite to say anything."

He killed Mrs. Elizabeth Allen and I dug her grave last night next to Henry Allen's on that small knoll just northwest of the cabin. Henry's dates were 1834 to 1873 and I put 1839 to 1875 on Mrs. Allen's. George said she'd just turned 36."

"How do we know you're not the one that killed her? We've just got your word for it," Matlock demanded.

"Well I am telling you about it and I don't have their horse. I wouldn't have told you anything if I was a murderer. I'd keep my mouth shut."

"That makes sense, Pa," Tucker said.

"And I'm telling you, those tots are in danger. The man's a homicidal maniac," Ay shot back.

What's a homicidal maniac, Mama?" inquired Helen.

"A killing madman. Now stay quiet."

"That's the reason I've got to get on after him. Something may happen to them before I can get there. They can lose their usefulness for all kinds of reasons or he just might decide to get rid of the boy and keep the little girl. I can see the boy is much more trouble to him. Oh yes, George told me the Kiowas killed his father."

"How do we know he didn't tell you this just before you killed him?"

"We're back to square one," huffed Aymond in frustration. "I wouldn't have known all of this burial and death stuff if I hadn't been digging a grave. I need to start after Arnold."

"Well, I don't know about that. You're a mighty fast talker. No telling what the truth is."

"Yes and while you talk, that murdering coyote is getting away and that will be your fault."

"Maybe you're right but you're goin' to take Junior and Tucker with you and they'll see the right thing is done."

"They can't both go. One of them needs to ride over and help George and take him a horse."

"I could do that," said Matlock.

"Who'll watch after your women folk? Spring's coming and the Indians are beginning to move. It might be safe but you can't take a chance."

"Ma and us can handle guns real good," said little Jenny. "Mary's a better shot than I am."

"I can shoot too," little Helen piped up. They all laughed.

"Go ahead, untie him. Tucker, you and Junior go with him. I think the girls can hold out all right until I get back with George Allen. We don't usually have any trouble with the Indians. We give them a beef now and then and occasionally a horse. It really pleases them when we run across a mule for them. They think they're delicious. Generally they leave us alone. No problems around since the Kiowas got old Allen. Now Junior, you and Tucker watch him."

"We'll keep an eye on him, don't worry," Tucker said.

"Let's get moving. I had intended to let Old Gold rest awhile anyway but he should be up to some more ground covering before dark. How far is it to Haley's Crossing?"

"About eleven miles. As you've probably guessed, there's not much there: a dirty saloon, a general store, blacksmith and livery, boarding house and a sort of school building that works as a church, too; but not even a barber, bank, or lawman. We can make it just about dark," said Tucker.

The three started for the barn and corral. "Keep an eye out for any longhorns drifting west while you're out there you two. Head them this way when you're coming back," Matlock shouted after them. Then more quietly to the four inside, "I'm going to wait 'til tomorrow to go over and get George. I'd have to sleep outside if I start now and I don't see any sense in that. And I couldn't get back tomorrow anyway. I'll get a good night's sleep first."

"Daddy, I could ride over with you," Jenny offered.

"Oh no you won't, young lady. You'll stay right here and watch after your Ma and sisters."

Things quieted down as they gathered at the window and watched the three men head west.

CHAPTER 4

DUSK FELL AND THE WIND PICKED up as it blew in off the plains from the north in Arctic blasts. Winter was making its last stand. Jericho was still tired and plodded along slowly. The other two riders were moving better and had gone ahead. At first they had stayed behind Aymond to keep him in sight, but the tiredness of Old Gold reassured them that the worn out horse was not going to run off anywhere.

"How much farther?" Aymond shouted ahead.

"About three miles," came back from Tucker.

"It'll be totally dark by then." Snow had begun to fall faster and heavier, making it difficult to see. "Do y'all know the way well enough to get us there in the dark or should we stop and make camp?"

"Junior and me can do it," Tucker replied, "There's an arroyo that runs almost the rest of the way. It'll keep the wind off too."

Bearman took his reins and tied them to the saddle horn, removed his gloves and shoved them in his pockets and put his hands under his armpits inside his coat. Shortly he could feel them tingling as the warmth came back into his fingers. The other two had been riding encased in blankets around their coats and seemed to be comfortable.

As they reached the outskirts of the tiny settlement they saw lights in a few windows. "We're going on to the boarding house to warm up and see if Arnold's still here. It's the second lighted window. You can catch us there." They took off at a trot leaving Bearman behind. Ay trudged on, finally bringing Jericho to a halt in front of what looked like a livery stable.

"Well Old Gold, you've made it. Let's get you rubbed down and fed." He banged on the livery doors and yelled. Finally an oil lamp appeared illuminating a face above it.

"Come on in. It's too cold to talk."

"Can you curry old Jericho here and feed him?"

"Sure, four bits."

"Done. Is the saloon still open?"

"Sure is, judging from all the noise coming from down that way just a few minutes ago. Usually stays open 'til way past midnight."

"Did a man with a couple of kids come through today?"

"Sure did. Ate something at Aunt Mildred's and pulled out about mid-day. Headed north."

"Thanks. Here you go," tossing over a cartwheel.

"Here's your change, mister," taking out a half dollar.

"No, you keep it and take good care of old hoss. He's some beat."

"Gee thanks, mister. He'll get extra special care."

Ay wandered off towards the saloon. The bat wings were folded back and a heavy door of rough timbers was closed. It opened easily to the touch and Ay stepped in and shut it behind him. Warm air engulfed him. He walked over to the cherry red potbelly and stuck out his hands and then rubbed his nose. Several hard cases turned from the bar to take a look.

He knew he looked young and could make a natural target for over-zealous fun from besotted minds. It had happened in the past and it did not really bother him. He opened his sheepskin lined coat so his Colt was available. The Winchester was at the stable. He was well aware from what the Matlocks had said that this was a wide open operation with no local law enforcement. His hands were getting warm and he rubbed his nose again and realized this was a mistake when it got an almost instantaneous reaction.

"I could take it once but I'm not going to let a snotty nosed kid come in here and keep spreading his crap all around this place, Get your ass out of here." The others looked and laughed. Aymond turned slowly and looked steadily at the hulking figure.

"Must have been a bully all his life," Aymond thought, "judging from his size." Aymond continued to stare at him, but said nothing.

"Didn't you hear me, you little fart. I don't like snotty nosed kids slobbering all over the place. Get your ass out now." Bearman eased his way around the stove until his back was to the wall and he could see everyone. He took in the fact that some thought it funny but would want no part of any action. Some others did not even think it funny. He registered the information that only the loudmouth and his unshaven crony on his left were the ones to watch. Still he said nothing and continued to look. "I said get your ass out and I won't say it again."

"I don't believe you will," Aymond said quietly. "You best go back to your drink before you buy yourself more trouble than you want." The hulk pulled up but saw only Ay's youth and not power. "Why you little punk!" He started forward swinging a huge fist at Ay's face. Ay could get the telegraph message from miles away and without decoding. He ducked down and came up under the extended arm with his hand tight and fingers together. It rammed into the Adam's Apple with controlled fury aided by the momentum of his attacker. The hard case's eyes crossed and he sank to the floor with his hands at his throat, turned sideways and passed out. His partner was pulling a gun when Bearman's Colt barked and put a bullet through the man's right foot. The gun banged on the floor as the second man collapsed. Ay looked around the room and saw no one else interested in quarreling. He holstered the Colt and put his hands back over the stove.

"Look what you've done to my foot. It's almost gone."

Bearman said carefully and clearly, "It could have been in your gut."

"There's no doctor in this lousy louse hole," the bully continued.

"Should of thought of that before pulling on your iron. You made your own bed. Leave quiet people alone from now on."

I'll get you, you little thwirt, just a shit ass bastard." Aymond reached down and picked up the hard case's pistol, turned it toward him and cocked it. "I didn't mean it. I didn't mean it. Please mister."

Ay lowered the hammer and passed the gun butt first to the barkeep. "Please put this away and don't return it until he's sober." The first of the would-be tough hombres began to stir and Ay removed his pistol and handed it across the bar with the words, "Add this to your collection. I'd like a little Tennessee whisky if you've got it or Kentucky if you don't."

"I'm sorry but the best I can do right now is a little Irish rye."

"That'll have to do." Bearman put a dollar beside the bottle after the drink had been poured. The bartender placed a handful of silver back. Bearman slugged it down, grimacing from the fact it had never been near rye much less Ireland. It would have to do whatever it was. It did have sting. Ay had hoped to savor the second glass slowly but slammed it down instead.

"Have you seen a man with two kids?"

"Nah, fella came in and said he had two head of kids feeding down at Aunt Mildred's. But I never saw'm. He bought a bottle, drank a little and took it with him. Ask Jake down at the stable or Aunt Mildred."

Ay looked at the two on the floor and glanced around the room. There was no hint of hostility. He ambled out closing the door quietly and headed for Aunt Mildred's which he had correctly identified as the second lighted window. He knocked and a good looking middle-aged woman answered the door. "I hear you feed well here and a couple of my partners came on ahead."

"They're inside. Come on in. I'm Aunt Mildred. Don't want to let all the heat out."

"Yes'm." Ay could see the two Matlock's pulling in the grub and he settled beside them.

"Damn good steaks," allowed Tucker, which, judging from the action, Ay believed.

"I'll have one too, please. With the fixings." Turning to Tucker, "Apparently they were here and moved right on."

"We found out from Aunt Gertrude that the kids ate here. Didn't say much. Very quiet," Tucker said.

"Well, it's too late and cold to follow them now. We'll get a quick start in the morning. Any place to sleep around here?"

"Aunt Mildred has let us have a room with two big beds. Ought to do."

Quiet followed for a spell and having finished up, Ay said, "Well I'm for bed. Yawl coming?"

"Not yet, me and Junior gonna go down and get a few drinks and find out what we can. Go on to bed."

Ay, went into the bedroom, sat down on the bed and took off his boots and hung his gun belt on a bed post. He took out the gun, ejected the spent cartridge and loaded another and put the gun under the covers. He removed his pants and shirt, pulled the blankets up and was soon asleep.

— — —

Aymond awakened to the noise of the two Matlocks cussing him and pushing revolvers in his face.

"What the hell is going on now?"

"Pa was right. You're just a trouble maker. Shooting up the place before you're here five minutes. Pa was right."

"Oh damn, Don't you two ever get the full story first? The guy took a swing at me and the other one was drawing. What am I supposed to do? Play dead?"

Yeah, well one almost has his neck broke and the other one could lose a foot. What in the hell did you do?"

"I just ducked his swing and stabbed him with my hand. I didn't want to hurt the other fellow bad so I just shot him in the foot. I could have killed him. It stopped all the fighting."

"Well Mike says you shot him for no reason at all. Said you told him to dance and then shot him in the foot when he didn't do it fast enough and then you hit Jeff in the throat with the barrel of your pistol when he told you to leave Mike alone." Tucker looked mighty upset.

"Now see here," said Ay, "He gave it to you all wrong. Didn't you ask the barkeeper?"

"Bar was shut up. Only them two was down there. They were hobbling to the blacksmith who is letting them stay there 'til morning. There ain't no doctor here."

"It didn't happen the way they said. They were coming for me. Anybody in there could tell you."

Why was it shut up so quick, huh? Pa sure was right when he said you had a slick tongue and to watch out for you. Well you ain't getting out of our sight. Tie him up, Junior. We ain't goin' to let him go nowhere." Ay was spread-eagled to the bed with arms and legs stretched out and tied to the four posters.

"Reckon he'll stay put now," allowed Junior.

"Now fellows, let's talk sense. You know I wouldn't do something like that. There's no reason for it."

"You're durn tootin'. That's why you're goin' to stay tied up 'til we figure what to do in the mornin'," said Junior. "Let's get some shuteye."

CHAPTER 5

AYMOND DID NOT SLEEP WELL BUT he had spent many nights under worse circumstances. Every time he tried to turn in his sleep, he jerked himself awake. He finally willed himself to stay still. He awoke with a cramp and tingling in his wrists and ankles. "Hey you two hootenannies. Wake up and untie me."

Tucker stirred, turned and opened his eyes to squint at Ay. "We ain't about to untie you, you no-good. We're going to take you back to Pa after breakfast."

"You can't do this to those kids. We need to get on their trail as soon as we can. Come on, untie me."

"You ain't goin' nowhere. Get up, Junior. Let's go get some flapjacks. You stay quiet and we'll bring you some."

"For Christsake, use you heads for something other than a food receptacle. Check the shooting out first."

"First things first," replied Tucker. "We'll get some grub and see how those two nice fellows you beat up are doin'."The two tramped on down the steps while Ay fumed. He realized yelling was not going to help him so he just stretched out as best as he could and relaxed. Fuming was not going to do him any good either.

Junior returned with pancakes and sorghum. He untied one of Ay's hands and said, "Now don't try anything. Here's your grub." Ay balanced the plate on his stomach and downed the cakes in no time flat.

"Now untie me and let's get after those kids."

"You're crazy. Put that arm back over here and don't make me get out the gun. I might show you what it feels like to get shot in the foot." Ay stretched back out and Junior secured the arm. "We'll be back after a while."

"Don't be gone too long. I need to go to the loo."

Junior went noisily back down the steps.

Finally, when it seemed most of the morning was gone, Aymond heard footsteps coming up the stairs and down the hall. The door opened and there were Tucker and Junior looking rather sheepishly around the edge. "I see you've found out the straight of it, you two idiots. Come on and turn me loose so we can get moving." Junior shuffled over and took the cords loose.

"Tell me what you found out," said Ay as he pulled on his pants and shirt.

Aunt Mildred said that they're just two no-goods who jumped you. And the guy at the saloon said they sure had it coming for starting after you like they did. I'm sure sorry, Ay," put in Tucker

"You sure are," Ay reposted. "Come on let's get moving," as he fastened up his gun belt. "You lousy so-in-so's made us lose almost the whole morning." They hurried to the stable, saddled and headed north.

About two miles out the tracks turned west and headed toward a small cabin at the foot of a hill. There were no signs of activity except several horses were nervously cavorting as they pulled up to the corral. The three dismounted and tied their mounts to the corral gate and looked around. The inside of the small barn showed nothing unusual and Ay went to the cabin and knocked on the door. No response. He banged louder. Still nothing.

"Anybody home?" from Ay as he pushed open the door. He expected no response and got none. He looked around and saw the humped up covers in the bunk, went over and pulled them back revealing a woman with her face and side of her head smashed in.

"Oh my God!" squealed Junior. "She's dead."

"She sure is," agreed Ay as he replaced the covers. "Junior, you ride back in to town and let somebody know and come on back here as soon as you can. Tucker and I will look around and see what else is wrong. Get moving!" Junior took off in a rush while Tucker and Ay with guns out made the slow rounds of the cabin looking everywhere. There was not enough room for much to be out of sight and the search revealed nothing. They then went outside and found that Cain had picked up one more horse and the tracks of four animals left the compound heading north. "He's got a one track mind," murmured Aymond. "Always starts north." Then louder, "Let's get a grave dug so we can leave when Junior gets back. She's been dead since last night, so you idiots didn't cause it by your stupid delay this morning."

"Ah, Ay, yu got to 'mit that it didn't look no good of you doin' in them two dudes so quick. How was us to know?"

"Oh come on, let's dig that grave." It was finished before Junior got back with several townspeople and Aunt Mildred. Ay showed them the body and the tracks leading out.

"Y'all take care of the services while we take off after that murderer."

"My God. Look at her face and head," said Mildred, pulling back the sheet.

"How do we know you didn't do it?" came from the bartender.

"You don't, except we're telling you about it and Aunt Mildred knows we were at her place all night. This woman's been dead a spell. Body not even warm. Y'all take care of her and we'll go after that murdering bastard."

"Well, I'm not so sure," injected the barkeep again.

"George, you tain't got the sense of a centipede," from Aunt Mildred getting control of herself. "Them fellows were at my place all night and I can hear a cockroach walk. They left well after noon. And now you're carrying on like a blamed idjut! Molly's as cold as a plucked chicken. She's bound to have been dead a good while. She didn't start home 'til after these fellows came in. In fact, she was was 'miring that young'n, Aynond, e'en tho he do walk with a limp."

"Well, I guess you're right Aunt Millie. Sorry fellows but seeing Molly dead shook me up some."

"No offense Mr. Dunn," Aymond injected. "It certainly isn't pleasant but Tucker and I finished a grave while Junior was getting you. It's all ready out back. See to it she's read over proper and we'll get moving."

"We'll do that. Y'all get that damned murderer."

Ay and the Matlocks mounted and headed north at a fast pace. "He's going to turn west again so watch for the turn," as they continued along at a fast trot while taking in the tracks. Sure enough the turn was easy to spot even though Cain had tried to ride across rock to hide it.

"I sure can't understand that Mr. Arnold. He looked like such a nice man," mused Junior. "Yet look what he done to that poor lady You're right Ay. We've got to catch him. I guess you kinda think we're a couple of rumheads. Shor am sorry we gave you a hard time. Won't Pa be surprised when he finds out."

"Well, at least y'all let me get moving and that's something. I can see it's a rough tale to swallow but we can get him now."

The temperature had been rising and although the sky was still overcast, there was a hint of warmth in the air. Winter had done its worst and was surrendering to spring. But the rain that was starting was not helpful. It was beginning to wash out the tracks. Ay continued doggedly westward in the blind.

— — —

His quarry was not so dumb as Ay had thought. He may not have much intelligence but he had animal cunning. He waited until the rain was strong enough to blur the hoof prints and then made a gentle swing to the south. He continued for many miles until the little girl started crying. "I'm wet and I'm hungry."

"Keep quiet and no sniveling. You'll get to eat soon enough but if you give me any sass I'll slap your teeth out and make you walk." There was a silence from the girl. Little Sally had long since learned that she was paddled hard when she did not do as she was told and was given candy canes and cookies when she did exactly as instructed. She behaved. Arnold knew he did not have to worry about her in front of other people.

Joey gave him some concern, though. He was unruly and rebellious, but a few good whompings had brought him in line. He had tried to get some help from the people in the little town but Arnold had handled it easily.

"Little Joey here is still a might scared. The Indians killed his ma and pa, my brother. Lucky I had the kids over at a mine site when it happened. We'd been done in too. Little fellow thinks if we had been there we could've stopped it. But there was no way. War party must of had forty men and there were just the six of us. Real lucky we weren't there. Young fellow blames me though since we weren't there to fight the Indians. I know how he feels but he'll understand better when he gets older. Now he's so upset he says all kind of wild things. Hits me with his fists and says I killed them. Hurts to see him acting that way. Kinda knocked out of his right senses, but he's showing signs of getting over it."

This same talk with minor variations was used by the murderer on almost everybody they met. And it worked. People sympathized with the nice but disturbed kids and their kind uncle and wanted to do what they could to help. Arnold used it for all it was worth and got many a free meal and beds. He always slept with the kids. He had a special halter for Little Joey which he attached every night and secured to his wrist. He was careful to see that Joey had no access to a gun or knives and had threatened Joey once that if he made any real trouble he would hurt his baby sister. Joey believed him and this placed an additional shackle on the youngster.

The three of them rode on in the rain. Cain wanted to get as far south as he could while his tracks were being wiped out. He knew that anybody after him would know he was headed west and probably would look that way. Now he had a chance to shake off any pursuers if there were any. They trudged on south and the little girl began to whimper again.

"I'm hungry and I'm cold," Sally protested loudly.

"All right then, we'll stop for a little while and get you something to eat but we've got to keep moving." He lowered himself from his saddle and went back to the packhorse where he dug out a can of peaches. Pulling out his Bowie knife he sawed open the top and poured some of the juice and a half section into a tin cup and handed it to Sally. She drank some of the juice and pulled out the peach half with her grimy fingers and started eating eagerly, enjoying the sweetness. Arnold gave two halves and some juice to Joey who

41

gulped them down. Arnold finished the rest himself.

Darkness was coming on and it was getting colder. He dug out a bed blanket and wrapped it around Sally. "This'll keep you warm so you can sleep a bit as we go on. Grab yourself one too, Joe. Might as well stay warm. I don't want you sick." Cain took off his slicker, pulled on his fleece lined coat and got back on his horse. He draped the slicker around his shoulders. "Now, let's get moving." He headed on south and veered a little to the east.

CHAPTER 6

THE MATLOCKS MOVED RAPIDLY BEHIND
Aymond who suddenly slowed, came back along side them and said:
"It's beginning to get dark and I haven't seen hair or hide of the
tracks in some time. The trail's just washed away. I thought I saw a
hoofprint back there but I'm not sure. We'll just have to keep pushing westward and maybe edge a little to the north." Ay had misread
his man. The distance between them and their quarry increased.

Ay was stumped. He and the Matlocks had continued westward
and found no signs. They turned northward and back to the east
but still no signs. The Matlocks were growing tired and bored. In
every town or village it was the same: no man with two kids had
been through. Occasionally someone would add that he had heard
of such from a drummer while talking during a poker game but did
not know where or when he had seen them. It looked like a dead
end.

One morning Tucker said, "Ay, me and Junior is goin' back home.
We ain't gittin' nowhere here and Pa is gonna be worryin' about us."

"It sure looks like we let him get away. Can't think how. When
you taking off?"

"Probly 'morrow mornin'," Tucker said. "We'll put together some
vittles and head back. Won't Pa be surprised to learn what a mean
man that Arnold was? Shor fooled us."

"Well I'm not giving up. Only thing left is for me to swing south
and see if he went that way. Lots of desert south and west of here
but he could have gone toward Santa Fe. I'll just meander on down
that way and see what happens. He could have doubled back east.
I'll try that next but I feel in my bones that man was bent on going
west."

After the Matlocks left the next morning, Aymond bought a pack mule, some extra canteens and supplies and headed southwest. He arrived at the Pecos and followed it south a while but no one in the settlements or scattered cabins had seen a man traveling with two children. It was like they had vanished. He turned again westward and headed toward the distant hills.

— — —

March had moved rapidly to June and the summer sun was making itself felt. Dust was caking in the wetness of Ay's sweat. He was not familiar with this particular section of the world but had heard the tribesmen describe it and he remembered tales of the waterholes and tanks. Indian children learned young and well the necessities of survival and Three Trees had been bright and retentive. Now Aymond Bearman recalled that lore and tales. He dredged from his memory the landmarks and conditions of this area. Comanche and Apache had both traveled it.

He spotted the treble mesas that telegraphed the presence of large water filled tanks until late August and headed toward them. He gradually veered toward the southernmost of the three. They were much farther than he had supposed and it was late afternoon before he arrived in their shadow The shade relieved him from the oppressive heat. He had learned young to endure thirst and heat but still relished the coolness when it came. His water supply was now more than adequate. He stopped, dismounted and poured a healthy amount from his canteen into his broadbrimmed felt and offered it to Jericho. It disappeared quickly.

He did the same to Joshua, his light-hearted name for the wayward mule. He had never been able to get Joshua to march the whole way around Jericho. Ay finally gave in. Joshua was a faithful follower. He just did not want to lead. Ay knew when he was whipped and took the easy way out. It worked. That contrary mule kept up real well. Just don't try to push it in front. Unlike the horse, Joshua indicated his desire for more water by trying to suck the top of Ay's hat. Ay complied and the mule seemed satisfied with his second serving.

Ay took a big pull from the canteen, climbed back on Jericho and moved westward to the south edge of the butte enjoying the moisture dripping from his hat. Later on he stopped when he saw some bees heading north, jumped off, and followed them with his now empty canteen. He climbed about thirty feet and found the tank up under an overhang. He checked the water, found it warm but clear and good. He filled his canteen, climbed back to his mounts and unloaded three other canteens. He offered drinks to both Old Gold and Joshua and both took more. After they had enough he poured one over his head and the other two on the animals. They enjoyed their impromptu shower and shook themselves off. Ay laughed at his good sprinkling. It felt glorious.

All the canteens were full. Ay did not believe that a desert crossing required a low ration of water and four topped-off canteens could cover almost any situation. This was one way he differed from his Indian mentors. When he traveled he kept the canteens separated. He set them down and climbed higher until he could see far in both the direction he was going and behind him. He always liked to watch his back trail as he never knew when some unwanted visitor would show up and additionally, it was a good idea to know how the way back would look when returning. It was a useful habit learned from the Indians. Nothing was in sight in either direction. He remained still for some time to catch signs of movement but the desert was still. Ay relaxed some. He did not want to meet Comanches, Apaches or Comancheros, the latter were too much like Cain. These outlaw westerners or Mexicans traded with the red man. Not that this was bad, but Comancheros traded mostly in firewater and firearms. Any of the three outfits were bad news for a lone man in the desert. A man traveling by himself just naturally avoided company with other horsemen if he could. It made for a longer life.

He decided to stay where he was for the evening. He moved some distance away from the tank but went higher up following an easy slope the animals could make and which afforded a good view in every direction but with plenty of boulders for protection if he needed them. He stripped the saddle from the horse and the pack from the mule and hobbled them in a small patch of grass near a water seep.

Behind a circle of rock he made a small fire, put on his skillet and coffee pot, and watched the sun turn orange with red fingers reaching out into the almost cloudless sky. Three Trees enjoyed the solitude and quietness he had experienced often in his childhood.

He sliced off some bacon from a slab and plopped it into the skillet while the pot along side began to boil. The coffee was muddy and black, the way he enjoyed it. Even the grounds were tasty. Most people muttered and shook their heads when Aymond performed this stunt in public. He speared the bacon with his knife and savored the flavor. He dropped the last of his bread into the skillet to cook in the bacon drippings. He felt this sort of food rivaled any gourmet feasts he had partaken of in the East.

Having satisfactorily finished off the hunger, Ay settled back with his head on his saddle and began to think nice thoughts of the daughters Matlock. He could clearly envision young Jenny with her direct look and slight smile and Mary with her mischievous grin, much like little Helen's. Squirming some with half-erotic thought, he took himself in hand and went contentedly to sleep.

CHAPTER 7

AYMOND AWOKE WITH THE SUNRISE. He had been in no particular hurry to start and had taken no measures to ensure early awakening now that the Matlocks were not around to disturb him with their uneasiness. Looking around carefully, he made certain he was alone. He scanned the horizon rapidly and then again slowly. No hint of movement. Holding his vision steady, he checked peripherally, and repeated this in several directions. Again, nothing. He relaxed, convinced his first impression of nothing on his trail or in front of him was confirmed, being accutely aware that movement showed no matter how well camouflaged.

Stretching back, he put his arms behind his head and took in the morning sky. He enjoyed the big fluffy cumulus clouds and drank up the marvel of the smaller ones just shrinking and disappearing. It was as though God was putting on a magician's vanishing act. His thoughts of Jenny and Mary returned bringing a smile to his face and then he realized that he felt tired for the first time in a number of days and discouraged for the very first time.

"What am I doing up here?" he thought. "I'm wasting my time now."

Aymond had trailed many miles without slowing down and in all that distance had caught not even the slightest whiff of the fugitive and two youngsters. He had telegraphed Doc Bearman in Lizard Sands the first time he had come across a town connected to a telegraph system. Having alerted Doc to look out for young George Allen and giving brief details, he had followed that short message with a long letter setting out everything and letting Doc know that he would not be able to give him a forwarding address. He had followed up with several short letters when he came across a stage coach station or a small settlement with a post office.

He wondered what could have happened to the brute. Indians or Comancheros could have killed him and carried off the children. Ay had heard of no unexplained killings or Indian attacks, so the rascal was not up to his old tricks anywhere in the vast area Ay had covered. He was beginning to feel maybe he should go on to Lizard Sands and listen there for reports of odd killings.

Making up his mind instantly that this was the thing to do, he sat up and surveyed his surroundings one more time very carefully. He got up, put the pack on Joshua, the saddle on Old Gold, and jumped aboard. He was going back to Lizard Sands—straight in, but he was leaving room for the pleasant contemplation of Jenny and Mary.

CHAPTER 8

LINDSEY BENEDICT HAD FOOLED AY WELL. While drinking in a back water saloon Cain had picked up a loose woman and they had traveled on as a family. The four attracted no unusual attention or comments and had blended into the background. He took on the new handle of Willy Sharpe. He thought it sounded good with Mrs. Gertrude Sharpe. Buying a second hand wagon, they traveled around a while and ended up in Boonetown where Arnold landed a job as a back-up bartender. He did the cleaning up, sweeping, toting, and all the disagreeable jobs. On busy nights he helped dispense the alcohol. Even though he was constantly bitching to himself and Gertrude, he did what he was told and the boss was reasonably pleased.

Arnold always kept his ears open. He knew he could not stand the present situation long and he tried to figure out a way to pick up plenty of cash without much effort before leaving. He eyeballed the folks coming through and talked his woman into taking a parttime job at the eatery to pick up information from the parties passing through.

Arnold was not interested in the trail hands or ranch workers. He wanted a soft touch like greenhorns looking for the promised land with a little something stashed somewhere. He encouraged Gertrude to keep her ears open and to report to him all likely strangers. Gertrude sensed he did not mind being on the shady side of the law, so she did not object to his untoward conduct so long as it did not involve her and she could get her share of the loot. She was not fond of slinging hash and cleaning up after sloppy eaters and was anxious to move on to some place like New Orleans or San Francisco with money to burn. She did what she could to ferret out nuggets of information without being too obvious. Western women liked to gossip and exchange news, especially while on the move and almost any were ready to broadcast their dreams and plans to anyone who would listen. Gertrude listened carefully and passed the information on.

Gertrude had even gotten fond of the two kids who had taken up with her as a sort of foil against Cain. He did not yell as much or beat on them when she was around. He had hit the boy once when he was drunk and she had turned into a tigress protecting her young and slammed him with a hot skillet. She did not know why she did it; she just liked the kids. He backed off immediately but brooded about it and decided he'd get his revenge but not yet. He had a good thing going and wanted to keep it that way.

Several times when he had learned that a passing wagon had money or other valuables on board he had sneaked around while the parties were in town and relieved the vehicle of some of its cargo. He kept the loot out on the plains in a spot he had found until the group moved on. They did not always discover their loss right away and the town people seldom heard of it. Those who did complain got no real help from the listening and sympathetic townspeople, who, on a number of occasions, included Gertrude in their midst.

Arnold was good at taking things even from wagons tied up in front of the general store. He had gotten compliments from the boss for keeping the front of the saloon so tidy. His saloon generally did not attract the riff-raff who could usually be found down the street. Arnold, with his broom and sack sweeping away in the street, was a usual sight and attracted no real attention. When he was sure the street was empty he could fill his sack from the available buckboards and wagons. He was careful to avoid taking things from locals unless it was something that would not be missed immediately. He watched as provisions were brought out and items such as onions, potatoes, oranges, coffee and loose sugar provided him with cost-free edibles. Some people complained that the store was shorting them but most felt the kids or hands were latching on to the missing items. It was not enough to cause talk and no one ever suspected

Arnold. His drunken orgies were usually at home and Gertie could hold her own. It was only when they were soused at the same time that the noise attracted comment from the neighbors who worried about Joey and Sally. Since Gertie tried never to drink when Sharpe was at it heavy, it did not happen often.

On a number of occasions Willy Sharpe had learned of single wagons going through, looking prosperous, and with only one or two men. He would leave town with a pack horse saying he was going to try a little prospecting and made a point of heading toward some nearby hills. When out of sight of the town he would turn in the direction the settlers were taking and riding hard would overtake them. He would hold up some innocuous object like a skillet or hammer and come riding in. "You've left this," he would yell. The wagon stopped and Arnold would ride up and shoot the males immediately with his rifle before any hint of resistance was possible. He raped the women, being always careful to tie them first, and after slaking his desires, killed them. One amazon had almost finished him with a knife, which he barely escaped when she had slipped. He remembered it and took no chances.

Transferring valuables to the pack horse, he buried the dead and set up a marker with names if he knew them and dates that were off enough to provide him with an alibi. He found this worked better. People did not bother graves and later search parties, if and when they did come across the site, assumed it the work of Indians, Mexicans or bandits. Cain would burn the wagon and what was left and scatter the ashes removing all of the iron including the wheel rims. He had learned that Indians took all iron for arrow heads and other needed equipment.

The horses or mules he just turned loose. He knew that strange horses at his place would attract all sorts of comments They would join the mustangs herding in the area or wander back the way they had come. On one occasion two had meandered into Boonetown causing a search party to ride. They found the ashes of the wagon and the graves and decided it had been an Indian attack with some later party handling burials. They wondered why the Indians had not taken the horses. One of the group surmised, "Must have been grazing and run off during the attack." There was general assent. The word of the Indian attack began to spread over the area.

Generally Willy took the pack horse to his hideyhole and stashed the loot which was becoming substantial. He then returned to town from his "prospecting," cursing his luck and getting part tight at the saloon where he worked. He was shrewd and never gave anything away when in this condition. Gertrude would come and get him when he apparently passed out. She would wonder where he had been when he came back with more money than he left with but since he always gave her some she said nothing. His boss did not seem to mind as long as it did not happen too often.

After doing nothing in the way of looting in the time following the search party, Gertude told him of a German family that was passing through about twenty miles out. She had heard that the Germans wanted no part of Boonetown having mistakenly heard that the townspeople were rough on Germans. He rode out, found the Germans, two brothers and a wife, who were suspicious and on their guard. Willy had expected this and had ten pounds of sugar and five pounds of coffee in a poke tied to his saddle bags. He rode up slowly, with his hands up and palms forward, shouting, "Friend." The Germans allowed him to approach and he made some innocuous talk about prospecting in the area. They invited him to share their meal which he accepted and was served the leavings of buffalo meat in a stew with a few onions. They were drinking only water and he could tell their supplies were running low. When he was ready to leave he offered them the coffee and sugar which they refused and he said, "We have to share out here. People have helped me out when I needed it and I can tell this little lady would enjoy some coffee and sugar." Reluctantly they accepted the offer and insisted he dismount and share a pot with them. He did and then rode off leaving a friendly atmosphere. Two days later he returned with his rifle in front of him across his saddle. The Germans, who stood on the ground alongside the wagon, eyed him cautiously with their weapons in view.

"Heard there was Injuns around and I wanted to be shore you folks was safe." The party relaxed as he rode up and took a sack of potatoes from his saddle bag. "Here's some spuds fur ya." He leaned over and handed them to the woman on the wagon seat. She took them and placed them behind the seat. She was generous in her thanks. "Watch out for Injuns now," he said as he turned to leave. He rode a few yards away and then turned. "Oh yeah. I almost forgot." He dropped the lead to the pack horse, eased up the rifle, and shot both men in the chest. The woman screamed, stood up on the seat and tried to scurry back into the wagon to get her gun. Cain, who had started his horse forward while shooting, reached down and grabbed her skirt, pulling her back. He dumped her on the ground and jumped down. She still screamed. He slapped her across the mouth, raped her, then shot her in the head from behind, and dug two graves putting the woman and one of the men in. He pulled a board off the side of the wagon and carved their names, which he had made a point of learning while sharing their meal, and a date two days ahead.

He loaded the other body on the pack horse which he tied to the rear of the wagon alongside his mount, then got in the wagon and headed it for his hideyhole. After unloading most of their goods he took the wagon east toward some hills. He loosened the pack horse from the wagon and walked it over to a ravine; next he took the body of the other man from the pack horse and dumped it down into the ravine, tumbling rock down over him. His disappearance would let people think he had buried his dead and gone on with wagon and team.

Willy had found a blind canyon the last time out and he ran the wagon in and pulled it over to an overhang. He covered it with limbs and vines after removing the wheels and taking down the canvas top and supports. He shooed the four horses to the rear and worked a couple of hours to close in the canyon at a narrow spot. He went back to the wagon and retrieved the potatoes, sugar and coffee. Luckily they had not used much. Gertrude had heard he had bought the sugar and coffee and had wanted to know where it was. He had not answered in a direct way, just grunted and Gertie had raised hell. "Well, this'll get her off my back," he thought. "I'm running lucky."

One day Sharpe had a change of luck. He had grabbed a bunch

of oranges from a local buckboard and shoved them in his sack just as the ranch cook came out with a bag of potatoes. Unfortunately for him, Willy's sack had a damp bottom and the oranges broke through and cascaded over the ground. The cook looked down and saw the oranges and immediately checked the back of his buckboard. The orange sack was ripped up the side and it was obviously missing oranges. He tied into Willy immediately and the suddenness of the attack while scrambling to retrieve the oranges resulted in a stunned Benedict flat on his back and groggy. "I'll not have any petty thieves ransacking my wagon," the cook yelled as the noise attracted a number of people. "He was snitching my oranges," he continued to yell. Lindsey Benedict jumped to his feet and took off running towards his home.

"I've done it now," he was thinking. "How in the hell had that sack gotten wet?" He could think of no good reason and ran a little faster when the shouts behind him got louder. Turning into his shack, he jumped on the porch and through the front door. "I blew it, Gertie. They caught me taking some oranges."

"Get out the back way quick and keep the house between you and them. I'll handle it." She watched Willy run toward the creek and disappear down into the creek bed. There was a loud knocking and shouts of "Come out Sharpe, you bastard or we're coming in."

Gertrude went to the door wiping her hands on the flour sack apron she wore. "What's the trouble?"

"We're looking for that sorry husband of yours. He stole some oranges out of my buckboard and he came running this way."

"Oh dear, I'm afraid it's my fault. I was after Willy to get some oranges for the kids; they've got the sniffles and we have been short on cash. Oh dear, oh dear. He's not a bad man, Mr. Vernon; he's just not much force. Oh he went and took some. Oh dear, oh dear."

"Well, where is he? He came this way."

"He's not in the house Mr. Vernon. Y'all come on in and look." No Westerner would like to imply a housewife with kids would be untruthful in a situation like this so the crowd backed down on entering. "I'll pay you! I'll pay you for the oranges," she blurted as she turned to go back to the kitchen.

"Ah, that won't be necessary, Missus Sharpe. Them oranges is scattered all over back by the store. He didn't get away with them, so you don't owe for nothing. I'll get the oranges up. Please excuse me for bothering you ma'am." Vernon turned and walked away followed by the now quietened group. As Vernon rounded the corner toward the store he started gathering up the spilled oranges. After he had gotten four he turned to a boy in the group and said, "Here Tom, take these to Missus Sharpe and tell her they're for the kids. Now run on." Some in the crowd shook their heads, but most of the townspeople liked the Sharpe children. They were well behaved, remained quiet all the time, and never caused any trouble.

Mrs. Sharpe took them to church but did not let them go to school. "We don't believe in schoolhouse teaching. Kids do better if they're taught at home," she had often stated. Willy believed in keeping the children on a close leash where he could keep an eye on them. That was why they were allowed to go to church with Gertrude but kept out of school. They had learned their ABC's and could do their times tables but their reading was limited to two old books and the Bible. Sharpe liked to read to them out of the Old Testament and let them know what doom awaited them if they disobeyed. His thinking was that the Old Testament had many stories to subdue children. The two stayed subdued. The boy had troubling thoughts but learned to keep them to himself and not to give any difficulties. He was biding his time waiting on some better situation to develop. As it was, he and his sister were taken care of and Gertie saw to it that Willy did not hurt them. They had heard what Gertie said to the men but kept quiet. When Tom brought the oranges they ate them with no concern. They had gotten used to the current circumstances and child-like accepted them.

Some of the harder types in town disapproved of the way Vernon had let Sharpe off and sat huddled in the saloon. "I sure don't like this much. That thieving hound got off scot free. Old Hank Vernon shouldn't have giv'n in that easy. Missus Sharpe wadn't caught doin' nothing but that bastard sure was. We've been missin' other things around here and he must have been the one doin' it. We need to do something about it."

"Yeah, that lousy no good's been caging our stuff. That's where it's been goin'. What we gonna do?"

"It's all eaten up by now. Mostly bacon, flour and sugar. Ain't gettin' none of that back."

"Well, I mist a hammer and saw wunst. Betcha he's got 'em."

"We can beat the crap out of'm until he tells. He's got it coming anyway. Hank let'm off too easy. He'll have to come back tonight and then we can get'm."

"That's a great idea. We can meet back here after supper and then jump him."

"He's got it comin' the lousy bastard."

"Yeh, see y'all after supper."

CHAPTER 9

CAIN SNEAKED IN AS SOON AS IT WAS dark. Gertrude was putting the kids to bed. The little girl let out a sharp cry when she saw him but quieted immediately with a soft whimper.

"Well, I got it taken care of," Gertrude crowed. "Old Hank even sent the kids some oranges. You're goin' to have to stop taking things around here. We won't have that luck next time. But go on in and I'll get you supper. It's probably cold now anyway. Go on, I'll be in as soon as I finish here. She gave Sally a hug and tucked her in and saying good night to little Joey followed Willy into the next room. She ladled out some stew that was still warm and cut several pieces of cold corn bread. Willy ate rapidly.

"Guess I'd better get up to the Silver Circle. Sho hate to go but the boss'll fire me sure if I don't show up. We're goin' to have to get out of here. Start gettin' your things together but don't make it obvious if somebody comes. Sho hate to go down there. Willy moved slowly into the front room and out on the porch, stood for a few minutes and looked down the street. Not seeing anything he edged down the steps and started toward the saloon.

The mean ones were waiting. "Where in the hell do you spose he is? He should of been down here hours ago."

"Waitin' 'til it got dark more'n likely. He'll probly sneak in the back way." They went back to their poker game. "Do you really think he'll show up tonight?"

"Sure, he'd be afraid not to. Deal."

"Well he might just decide to take off."

"Not with over half a month's wages comin'. He'll be along."

Sharpe slipped in the back way, peeked around the corner, heard what was being said and was wondering how to handle it. The bar tender glanced up and saw him. "Get your ass in here, Willy. Where in th' ell have you been?"

Chairs that were leaning back dropped to the floor. Screeches came as other turned their chairs to look.

"Ain't been nowheres."

"You've gotta been somewhere. Get your ass in here and get to work. You think yo're gonna get paid by not working? Well you ain't!"

Cain went back into the storeroom and came out with the broom amd started sweeping at the end of the bar as far as he could get from the men watching him. He swept and swept while they continued to watch. Finally realizing he was going to have to come out in front of the bar, he came slowly around the edge sweeping vigorously. As if on command the six men at the poker table got up and stomped toward him.

"You lousy stealing skunk. We finally found out who's been taking our stuff and we've been blaming it on the kids or on John for not giving full measure. You lizard turd."

"You stinking bastard! We're goin' to stomp your friggin' brains out."

"I gits furst kick. He owes me," came angrily from the toothless miner.

Willy backed away. "Ah, fellas, I's juss doin' it cause the kids were poorly and hungry."

"Don't give us that load. You're taking home enough from here to take care of your family. You're just a greedy bastard."

"You've got it comin' and here it is." The toothless man's heavy fist crushed into the side of his head and another blow was thundered into his gut. As he started going down a blow under the chin straightened him back up, followed by a chop on the back of the neck sinking him to the floor. Boots started at his head and landed all over his body.

"Please fellas don't hurt me no mo."

"You got it coming," as a few more vicious kicks found soft spots to land.

58

"That's enough now," ordered Jake from behind the bar. "Don't kill him. They're six of y'all." The men drew back. Willy was out cold. "Leave'm there. I'll get him up." Jake put a couple of tumblers of water on the bar and walked around it. He picked up the glasses and dumped the water into Sharpe"s face. "Get up Willy." As the man stirred, the others looked, turned and settled back to their poker game. Jake reached down and grabbed a hand and pulled. Willy came unsteadily to his feet. "Now, let that be a lesson to you. Leave other folks' stuff alone." He helped Willy to the storeroom and settled him on a sack of sugar, had second thoughts and pulled him over to a rag pile. "You'd bleed on the sugar. Stay here 'til you feel better." Willy just moaned and lay in his drunklike stupor.

Later that evening he shuffled home. Gertie had expected it since some of the other women had passed the word.

"Come on in here and get cleaned up. My God, you're a mess. I've got hot water on and some clean towels. Man, they worked you over good."

"Shut up woman, I'm hurting," he howled.

"Shut up yourself," she shot back. "You brought this on, taking what wasn't yourn."

"Well you don't mind benefitin' from it. Get off my back," Willy growled at her as he pulled his torn shirt off and dumped it on the floor and dipped one of the towels in the hot water and lightly sponged his face and torso. He gradually got off most of the blood and grime. "We've got to get out of here, I can't take this no more. We'll pack and go tomorrow."

"Use your head, you moron. They're expecting that. They figure you'd cut loose and run. I've talked to the girls and they don't think you'll have any more trouble for a while if you don't cause none. If you start running they might want to know how come? And they might get wild again or figure something else. You just clean up and go to bed." Gertrude picked up his shirt, shrugged and tossed it in the dirty clothes hamper, got another shirt from the chest and put it on the back of the chair. "You'll feel better in the morning and we'll talk it over."

CHAPTER 10

"KEEP COMING, JOSHUA." AY PULLED AT the halter tied to the black mule and the recalcitrant animal begrudgingly increased his speed. Ay had found it tough going to get him into a trot. The easiest times came when there was a water hole ahead and Joshua was thirsty. He could sometimes get him moving with a switch across the rear but Ay was not comfortable with this procedure. He figured he could outsmart this mule.

Ay had heard at several stops that Indian attacks on travelers had started again around Boonetown and he wondered if Cain had surfaced. Must of the reports were definite that it was Indians. Even tales of gun battles from supposed survivors floated around. He was eager to get to the next town to find out what was happening.

He got into Potato Patch about dusk. It almost lived up to its name. A weed-choked garden with carrots, potatoes, radishes, egg plant and that new love apple, the tomato, was barely surviving on the near side of town. There were two saloons, a general store, no bank but a barber and carpentry shop combined. There was a smaller sign: "Funerals Handled."

His attention was immediately drawn to an affray in front of the farther saloon where four bruisers were beating up on a small man. "You young bastard! Scum! Stinking fart! Wretched ass hole!" and similar epithets were noisily forthcoming. Ay picked up his pace, tugged on Joshua and approached the melee. The figure was on the ground and boots were swinging and connecting. The figure writhed and moaned in agony.

"What's going on here?" Ay demanded.

"None of your damn business!" jumped at him.

"This young turd thought he could drink in the saloon with real men and wouldn't leave when told. We're teaching him some manners."

"Get your ass out of here or you're next. We're tired of you young farts trying to act like men. Get your ass on and leave us alone or I personally will stomp you next," Jake menaced while still kicking the prostrate figure.

"Well that's not right neighborly of you. What might you be called?" from Ay in a slow drawl.

"I'm Jake Hudson and you're coming off that horse." He quit booting to reach up for Ay but Ay was prepared. He grabbed Jake's wrist while turning Jericho. Jake stumbled forward and Ay pushed him down with a quick movement. Jake fell to the ground and Joshua, surprised by the movement, jumped forward and put his 1600 pounds on Jake's ankle. There was a crunch and Jake screamed. The others turned and Ay already has his gun out.

"Just stand easy and nobody else gets hurt," he said quietly with an air of authority.

One looked like he was ready to draw and Ay turned the gun toward him. He gradually moved his hand away from the butt and remained motionless. Another muttered, "You little snit. If you didn't have a gun on us, I'd pickle your toes." Ay looked at him and he stopped muttering.

"Get your friend up. He's going to need some medical help. Is there a doctor in this burg?"

"Hell no. We're lucky to have a barber. Sometimes he helps with the doctorin'. The carpenter's pretty good too. The nearest one is in Boonetown. Now look what you've done. Busted up a good man."

"Had the same thing happen to me. Should of kept his hands to himself. Wasn't intended but he had it coming."

"Well you just watch out. We'll remember this." They stooped and grabbed Jake under his arms and supported him while he hopped, groaning, toward the barber shop.

"You all right young fellow?" Aymond asked the still recumbent figure. "He's probably only a year or two younger than I am," Ay muttered bemusedly to himself and then louder, "That was beginning to be some tough whipping."

"I'll make it," in a whisper.

Aymond directed Jericho to the hitch rail in front of the saloon and dismounted. He threw the reins over the pole, glanced to see that Joshua was still secured and turned back to the boy. He stooped down. "Let me help you up. What you called?"

"I'm Cliff Jones. I'm up from Galveston. Headed west." He was still talking in a whisper.

"I'm Aymond Bearman, headed home to Lizard Sands. Feel like you've got anything broken?" he asked in concern.

"I'm not shore, but I shore hurt."

Ay ran his hands over his arms and legs and added, "Nothing broken that I can tell. Let me help you up."

"Not sure I wanna, but all right."

Ay, who was now behind him, reached his arms under his shoulders and lifted. After a yelp, Cliff came up with only a small moan. Ay steadied him while he stood.

"Where's your horse and where're you staying?"

"Horse's staked out and I ain't stayin' nowheres. Camp out mostly. Ain't got much money. Take odd jobs mostly for my grub and spendin' money."

"Well, let's get you back into the saloon for something to eat and drink. They won't bother you this time." Aynond half carried, half dragged the moaning boy through the batwing doors and settled him on the floor with his back against the wall next to a table near the front. The place was about empty except for five men playing poker at a round table in the back and the bartender.

The bartender looked up but the others paid no attention. "Ain't you had enough?" the bartender snarled and then to Aymond, "Why'd you bring him back in here? I've had enough trouble. Get him out! And I think you'd better leave too."

Ay turned slowly, looked long at the bartender and said, "We're staying. This youngster needs some help and sustenance and you're going to provide it. What do you have to eat?"

"I said to leave. You hard o hearin'? You're nuddin' but wet ears like he is. Now git!"

Aymond walked over to the bar, reached well across and grabbed the keep by his shirt front and pulled him forward across the bar until their faces were inches apart. "Give us a beer apiece and tell your cook to prepare some food immediately. And don't try any funny stuff with any six guns or shotguns under the bar. I can get a gun out quicker. Now move." Ay shoved him back against the shelves behind the bar. The bartender straightened himself up, turned and drew two beers and then scurried for the back room. Ay watched him go and then took the beers over to the table and settled in a chair. He leaned over and handed one to Chris. "Here you go kid. This will perk you up."

"I don't think I can handle it," said Cliff as he slowly raised his arm. It fell back. "Ain't used to beer." Ay held the schooner over and Cliff took a sip. He pushed the vessel away and, after a moment, put his hand back up to the bottom of the container and took a bigger pull. "Tastes funny but it really helps," he whispered.

Ay went back to the bar. He noticed that the poker players were watching now. He went behind the bar and picked up a wet cloth and spotted the omnipresent shotgun. He bent over and quietly opened it and took out the two shells and as quietly closed it. He slipped the shells in his pockets and walked out from behind the bar with the wet cloth and. in a voice slightly louder than necessary, said, "Here son, clean your face and hands off." He felt weird calling the youngster, son, but it seemed right natural. Ay was far advanced for his years.

Cliff tried to scrub at his face and then daubed on his hands and wrist. He was trying hard to make his arms go but could not. Cliff fell back against the wall. He was obviously marked up and ugly bruises were showing on his face and elsewhere. His breathing was fast and noisy. Ay gave him another swig.

"Let me pull up your shirt," Ay said as he loosened the boy's belt and tugged up the torn shirt uncovering more bruises. "How's it feel?"

"Horrible. It really hurts."

"Well, we'll get some grub in you and see what we can do to get you squared away."

As if on cue the bartender returned toting a large tray with ironstone plates holding big steaks and beans. Dumping the tray on the table, he mumbled, "Here."

Ay picked up one plate and slid it in front of Cliff. "Think you can handle this?"

"Don't know." Ay cut him a small piece and put it in the lad's mouth. The kid tried to chew but could not make it. "Jaw hurts."

"Bartender, bring him some soup and another couple of beers." Ay finished his mug and offered the boy another drag. Cliff took a healthy pull. Ay then drew his steak over and started eating slowly. He saw that the poker players were still keeping an eye on them.

The bartender returned with the soup and beers while saying, "I'd finish up fast and get out of here if I was you. That Jake and them boys ain't ones to fool with and they'll be back."

"Don't quite reckon Jake's going to trouble anybody for a while. Now the others might decide to get frisky but this boy needs a place to sleep. You got any rooms?"

"Nothing for you."

Looking him square in the eye, Ay repeated, "You got any rooms?"

Squirming under the stare, the bartender added, "Just a storage room with two bunks but I'd rather you two headed on. Don't want no trouble."

"We'll stay."

Ay spooned some soup into Cliff, who still had his appetite despite his injuries and weakness and was able to finish off the whole bowl. Ay gave him another pull at the beer, finished off his own second one, then stood up leaving about half of his meat on the plate having completely downed the beans.

The bartender from behind the bar growled, "I said I don't want you boys staying." He was holding the shotgun out of sight behind the bar. He was thinking, "That stinking kid ain't gonna get a chance this time. I can sho beat him now, treating me like some nigger." The poker players were watching.

Aymond sauntered over to the bar. "Stop right now, you young squirt," snarled the keep as he brought the gun up and pointed it at Ay.

Ay slowed, but continued on. "I wouldn't do that if I were you.

The deck's stacked against you."

The barkeep cocked both hammers but Ay did not stop. "I wouldn't try to pull those triggers. You might get in trouble. Bad trouble."

The bartender could see that Ay's hand was not near his gun butt. "Stop right there or you'll deserve what you get."

Ay was now edging down the bar towards the 'tender with his hands on the bar. "You're crazy old fellow. We just want a bed for the night with no trouble. This young man's in no state to travel. You can see that," with an attempt at logic.

The bartender saw the poker players watching. He did not want to be known as a dolt that backed down. "I warned you." But Ay continued. The barman pulled the trigger: nothing but a click! He looked puzzled and pulled the other trigger: another click. By now, he was backing away.

Aymond kept coming. "I told you the deck was stacked and I've no pity for bastards that try to kill me," as he eased his gun out of the scabbard and put it on the bar pointed toward the barkeep. He came on around the bar, reached over and took the shotgun from the keep and place it on the bar. He walked down the back of the bar looking carefully for any other weapons. He found a heavy pipe obviously filled with sand and an old converted Colt 32. It was a small gun, loaded. He tucked it into his belt and returned to the bartender. "Now what am I going to do with you? Do you need a minute or two to pray or is that beyond you?"

"Oh please, young man. I didn't mean no harm."

"Level down on me with a shotgun and you didn't mean any harm? You think I'm an idiot, too? Now that makes me more than a little mad. You just might have to die slowly."

"I'll scare the hell out of this no good and maybe he'll straighten up. He'd a killed me with no compunctions. He's a lucky bastard I'm not the killing kind but it's hard to control yourself after what he did," Aymond thought while keeping an eye on the players who only watched and made no move.

"Please don't kill me. I won't give no mo trouble," the bartender cried in a trembling voice.

Ay slapped him hard on the side of his face with his open hand. "Now that's what I want to hear, true repentance, not that crap you've been putting out. Now turn the other cheek as the Bible says." The bartender slowly turned his head and Ay slapped doubly hard on the other cheek with his left hand. "Now I'll just shoot you clean and not make you suffer."

The bartender started to go down on his knees when Ay grabbed him by the shirt and straightened him up. "It's possible you've really learned your lesson. Few more minutes of life won't hurt. I'll be right back," he said to Cliff as he shoved the cowering figure toward the back hall. "Now let's see our living quarters before you go." The barkeep began to make strange noises and indicated a door off the hall. It literally was just a storeroom but it had two iron bunks with straw mattresses and blankets.

"This will do fine. Now help me get Cliff in here." They went back to the main room where the players had resumed their game and tried to indicate they had no further interest in the proceedings. Ay figured they would cause no trouble and just kept them in sight.

The barman helped get Cliff up and into the back room and settled into one of the bunks.

"Give me the key," Aymond demanded of the bartender. He reached in his pocket and pulled out a ring, took a key off and handed it to Ay. "Let's go. Cliff, you rest easy and I'll try to find some medical help, after I've helped this lowlife to eternity in hell." He followed the barman out, pulling the door shut and turning to lock it, before pocketing the key.

"Please, young man, please. I didn't know what I was a doin'. Won't give nobody no mo trouble. Please, please.

"You're lucky I'm not a violent man. For now, we'll settle for the room. I'm not certain I'm doing the right thing, but you just stay on the straight and narrow and I'll mark it paid."

Taking the opened shotgun from the bar, Ay put the butt on the floor, jammed against his foot, and then put his full weight against the opened barrel and broke the gun into two pieces. Handing them to the barkeep, he said, "Nothing better happen to that young fellow while I'm gone."

"Don't worry, it won't." The bartender was subdued now and wanted nothing more than for Ay to disappear.

Aymond recrossed the barroom. Apparently, from their feigned indifference, the players were busy with their game, but Aymond could tell they were watching.

Aymond left them to their devices while looking out above the batwings. It was black outside. He pushed open the swinging portals and went quickly out. There were few lights showing but one seemed to be in the carpenter shop. He walked briskly down the boardwalk and looked in the small front window. The man inside was busily sawing a two by eight. No one else was in sight. Ay opened the door and went inside. The carpenter looked up in surprise.

"Sorry to disturb you at this late hour but I understand you do some doctoring."

"Mostly a carpenter now, with some burying on the side, but I 've done some bandaging over the years and had a short time in med school with some extensive practical experience during the war helping with the medics. What can I do for you?"

I'm Aymond Bearman. I've got a young fellow up at the saloon who's rather stove up and needs some attention."

"Oh, you're the one that tangled with Jake. He won't be tying into anybody for some time but those other hard noses will be after you and that kid. You'd do best to get out of these environs as soon as you can."

"Cliff can't travel. That's why I'm here. He's a tough little rascal but they squeezed him good. Not much juice left. He needs attention badly. More than I can give him. Certainly would appreciate your taking a look." Aymond had watched Doc Bearman patch up many a tough after a Saturday night brawl and had some knowledge of what to do but not that much hands on experience.

"Right. I'll go along."

CHAPTER 11

THE CARPENTER SET HIS SAW ON THE board, straightened up his project and went into the back room from which he emerged moments later carrying a small sachel and led Ay out the door. They moved briskly to the saloon. The poker players were still at it and one small cowboy was at the bar. The barman was evidently telling him the story of the fracas because he shut up as soon as Aymond entered. Aymond nodded and the bartender half nodded back. There were no signs of the bruisers. Ay headed for the back room with the carpenter behind him. He took the key from his pocket and opened the door. Cliff was sleeping.

"Hate to wake you up Cliff but the sawbones is here to take a look. Cliff this is ... I never did get your name."

"It's Brent Stephenson," wincing from taking in Cliff's broken appearance. "How you feeling?"

"Pretty lousy, Doc."

"I'm not a doctor but I do some doctoring. Let's get a look at you."

Cliff pushed at the sheet and Stephenson helped him get it off. Brent softly ran his hand over Cliff's blue and purple chest and abdomen. "Couple of cracked ribs and one has even separated. I've got some tape back at the shop. Pretty bad bruises and abrasions but they'll clear up with time. There's a rather bad and deep cut in back of your knee and shin. I'll have to sew it up for you. I'll have to go back to the shop to get the things I need. While I'm gone, ... did you say your name was Raymond?"

"No, Aymond, like in Amos."

"Oh, all right, Aymond. While I'm gone, get some whisky down the lad to relax him for what's coming. It's going to hurt some but it's necessary."

"Will do." He followed Brent out to the barroom. The barkeep was going at it again and, again, immediately shut up. Aymond requested a bottle of whisky.

Grabbing one from under the bar, the bartender too glibly said, "It's on the house."

"That won't be necessary," returned Ay. "How much is it?"

"A dollar seventy-five."

"Ay took two silver cartwheels from his pocket, putting them on the counter while saying, "Keep the change."

"And that's not necessary, young man," pushing out a quarter. "You helped get Cliff into the back room and, if you'll let me have a couple of glasses, please. Thanks." Aymond was hoping to defuse the situation. His anger was gone. He did not pick up the quarter.

He took the whisky to the storeroom, looked around and found a spare blanket, folded it up, put his arms carefully behind Cliff's shoulders and raised him while he slid the blanket under his shoulders and head. "How do you drink this stuff? Can you take it neat? "Just barely," said Cliff with a half-hearted attempt at a chuckle.

Ay poured out two big glasses and tendered one to Cliff. He was having trouble getting his arm up to hold it. "Let me help you. Just take a sip first. This bottle indicates it's some of that powerful Kentucky stuff. So just sip easy." Ay tipped up the glass slightly and let Cliff swallow. The boy almost gagged and Ay could tell he was not used to liquor. "Just take it down easy. We've got plenty of time." He was thinking it was not going to take much to get the youngster tipsy. He replaced the glass to Cliff's mouth, tilted it and encouraged him to take a bigger swallow. It went down with not as much fuss but Cliff looked like he was having trouble keeping it down. Ay took a slug from his tumbler.

He had downed a lot of straight whisky while at the University of Virginia. Joe Bearman, Doc's brother, had told him to "drink all you want but drink like a gentleman and don't get drunk." Aymond had taken this to heart and believed in it. He could always tell when he was getting close to the little red line and called a halt. He was a long way from the red line now. He could hold his liquor all right but he needed to be cautious in the current situation.

He could see that the boy was beginning to feel the effects. After a few minutes he encouraged him to take another large swallow. Cliff survived the dosage with fewer signs of distress.

"Almost there," Aymond thought. "Everything will be ready for Stephenson." He took another long pull from his own glass and realized he was feeling relaxed himself. "Better hold up. Some of that bad company may come back and I don't want to be a sitting target."

Stephenson returned with a satchel in one hand and tools in the other. He placed the tools on a storage shelf and the satchel on a near-by chair. He drew up another chair and sat down by his patient. "Guess we'll do the ribs first. How you coming with that whisky?"

"Puurrrty goood, Doc, heh, heh, heh," with a running giggle.

"Look's like you've helped his pain a great deal while I was gone. Should make it easier on him but this is going to hurt like hell," reaching into his bag and bringing out a roll of tape. "Here, hold him up easy while I get this stuff around him."

Aymond put his arm back under Cliff's shoulders and said, "Easy lad. Let's sit up."

"Suuurrre thiiiing Ayyyymond. Ooooooooh that hurts."

"Just hold on; it's going to get worse. Want some more whisky?" he offered.

"Suuurre thiiing Ayyymond."

Aymond put the glass to his lips and poured in a healthy amount. Cliff spurted and gurgled and some of the liquid hit Brent.

"Hold on here. I certainly don't need a whisky bath.

"Gaaaaave Doc a whiiiiskeeey bathy," giggled Cliff.

Brent did not think it amusing but was used to the situation. "Hold off on any more 'til I'm not in front. Here, grab this roll," shoving it around Cliff's back and then retrieving it from Ay. "Now this is going to hurt real bad. Do you want a bullet to bite on?"

"Suuiuurree thiiiing, Doc." Cliff was almost gone.

"Think he can hold it without swallowing it?" Ay enquired.

"Sure thing, Aymond." Brent laughed. "What he's going to feel will

70

make him think he's bitten it in two. Hold him up tight in the back now. I'm going to push hard." Stephenson extended both palms and shoved on Cliff's chest with great force. There was a grating sound and then a click, which was drowned by his loud, agonized scream. "That went a lot quicker and easier then I thought," Brent injected. Cliff settled down to a whimpering. "That must really have tortured him. Glad it's fixed. The other ribs aren't so bad. Now let's get this tape around him tight."

Having gotten the tape secured firmly, Brent said, "Let's take a break. I'll have some of that whisky myself."

Ay went out to the barroom and returned with another glass. He poured a generous portion for Steve and a like amount for himself. He downed a healthy slug and picked up Cliff's glass. "Think he can stand some more?"

"Ask him!"

"Want some more whisky, Cliff?"

"Suuuurrrre thiiiing, Ayyyyymmmmoooond," as Brent beat his hands in time with the slurred syllables. Brent laughed again.

"Wish they were all like this. Makes it easier on a man. Some of 'em make you want to throw up. But my puking ain't going to make it any better for a guy getting his leg sawed off." And more quietly, "Would rather saw a board 'cause it don't holler. Go on give him his poison."

Ay got another generous snort down his newly found friend. Cliff's head started drooping. "That ought to hold him. What's next?"

"Putting on the iodine. Started using this stuff during the war. Never lost as many to gangrene and other things as I did with whisky. But it stings like hell. Watch him start hollering again." Brent took out the glass dauber and applied the iodine thickly on the abrasions, at times slowing as he wiped dried blood away with a damp towel. Cliff did yell and kept yelling. The bartender walked to the door and looked in. Brent said when he saw him, "Just standard procedure for open wounds, Mac. He's just yelling louder than some. Nothing but iodine. Wait 'til I sew up the cut down here. Then you'll hear some hollering." The bartender backed out the door and disappeared. Cliff's yelps came to an abrupt halt as he passed out.

"Best thing for the poor rascal. Let's take another break. More of that nectar, please." The bottle was beginning to get low and Ay and Brent finished it.

"The youngster won't be needing any at the moment, so we can finish it off in good conscience."

"I'll get another," said Ay meandering out into the hall. He returned a few minutes later with a duplicate. "Those fellows still playing, Do they ever quit?"

"Goes on for two or three days sometimes. They catch naps on these bunks. You've done them out of their sleeping parlor,"

"Didn't seem to bother them."

"It won't 'til they get sleepy. But that set won't bother you. It's Jake's crowd you'll have to watch. Be late in the morning before they're up though. If you can find a wagon you could get Cliff out of here before they're stirring."

"Well, I'm headed for Lizard Sands. Think I could rent one for the trip and send it back by someone heading this way?"

"Mighty chancy, but the liveryman might do it with a hefty deposit. I would lend you mine but I'm always using it to tote lumber and coffins. Use it as ambulance, like on you. All kinds of things, and sometimes, three or four times a day. Try the liveryman."

"Think I will. What else is left?"

"Sewing up that cut. It's still bleeding slow but I won't need you. Go ahead. I'll have another slug first. This is ugly work and it calls for more iodine. Go on; I can manage it through."

"Where's the livery stable, Mac?" Ay knew at least part of the bartender's name. "Not that in this large burg it couldn't be found but it's dark though and I'd like to save some steps."

"Sure. Go out to your left, past the first two stores on the right. Go down the passage way on the other side of the second store and it's the building right behind. Can't miss it." The card manipulators were still at it. Ay looked over the batwings carefully from ingrained cautiousness. Nothing stirring, just darkness. He looked around for a horse that might belong to Cliff but could discern no obvious candidate. He then untied Jericho and Joshua and murmured to the first, "I'm sorry old hoss, but there've been pressing matters, but you're first now. He found his way to the livery shop but all the doors were locked. He pounded on the big ones and finally a sleepy voice asked, "Who's there?"

"Aymond Bearman. I need to settle in a couple of animals for the night and talk to you about a wagon." The liveryman opened one of the big doors.

"Come on in."

"I going to need oats and rubdowns, even for this old onery mule."

"That's six bits."

Ay pulled out another silver cartwheel and handed it over. "Keep it and do an extra good job. And I'm going to need to rent a wagon to take to Lizard Sands."

"That's a right fur piece. What you goin' to be needin' it fur?"

"Got an injured man. Can't make it on a horse."

"Wouldn't be that young whippersnapper Jake and his gang worked over is it?"

"Yep, that's the one."

"Don't know Sonny. That's a right rough crew and I don't know you. They might mess up my wagon or you might not bring it back."

"I'm not worried about them. And I can give you a deposit. I'd sent it back by someone we know, headed this way from Lizard Sands. A wagon is the only way I'm going to be able to get that boy home."

Is Lizard Sands your home? And you said Bearman's your name. Are you any kin to Doc Bearman?"

"I'm his son."

"Well, well. Doc gets down here every now and then when Brent can't handle the situation. So you're Doc's boy. Don't look much like him." Doc Bearman was short and roly-poly unlike the tall slim Aymond.

"Adopted, sort of."

"Well that's a different matter. Can't fail to take care of Doc's boy. I'm Joe Hughes. You go ahead, son, and I'll take care of your horses; er, horse and mule, that is, and that wagon will be ready in the morning. Even furnish you with Lizzy, a pretty fair puller. Now get on."

"But Joshua, that's my onery mule, can pull the wagon. Won't need another horse."

"Yeah, and who'll pull my wagon back?"

"Didn't think of that."

"Get on son. They'll be ready for you."

Ay returned to the saloon, where Mac was sitting astride a chair backwards watching the game. The small cowboy was gone. Apparently recent events had not taken away from the bartender's social standing. The players were still engrossed and only one looked up when Ay came in. He continued to the back room. Stephenson had apparently finished and was cuddling a glass with about a half-inch of amber liquid.

"Ah, back already. Well, he's stitched up and ready to go. Need your help to turn him over on his back. Didn't want to take any chances with those ribs. He should do all right. Only yelped once and then back under."

"How'd you do with Joe? No wagon, huh?"

"He's rubbing down my two pets. I couldn't see a cayuse that looked like Cliff's. You wouldn't know where it is would you?"

"Nope. What about the wagon?"

"Turns out he knows my dad over in Lizard Sands and was willing to take a chance with me."

"Who's your father?"

"Doc Bearman."

"Doc Bearman! You don't look one damned thing like Doc Bearman!"

"Kinda adopted."

"Oh, I see. Well have a drink and then we can turn your buddy."

Both refilled glasses and did not drink fast but steadily.

After a good stretch of time, Brent staggered up and shook his head, "Must have drunk too much. Haven't been imbibing much lately." He continued to shake his head to clear his vision. "I'm seeing two of everything. Won't do."

Ay had not consumed as much and was still together, even though relaxed and limp. He dumped a cloth into the water bucket and tossed it to Stephenson. "Here catch this. Wipe your face off;

it'll help." Brent scrubbed away and looked up. He was seeing normally again but his head was beginning to hurt.

"Let's get Cliff turned, so I can get some sack time. I sure need it now." Together they got their arms under Cliff and gently turned him on his back. "I'll stick a blanket under his knee. It should help some." After getting the boy squared away, Brent headed for the door. "Keep this thing locked. Those are some mean bastards you've tied into so don't take any chances." Brent headed out and toward the barroom.

Aymond closed the door, picked up one of the chairs and tilted it under the knob. He turned the knob and yanked. The chair held. He then turned the key in the lock. There were no windows. "Well, that ought to keep us. I can hear any noise they'd make to get in." He took off his gun belt, shirt and trousers, took out his pistol and placed it on the head of the bed, turned back the blanket and crawled in. It felt great, and he felt safe. Stretching out, he wondered briefly where Cain might be, then he succumbed to his weariness and was fully asleep in seconds.

CHAPTER 12

IN BOONEVILLE FOLKS HAD FINALLY ALL agreed that Gertrude was all right. The kids too were good kids but the ladies attributed that to Gertrude, not knowing of Willy's stiffling control. But the murmurs against Willy continued to grow.

"Why should we have to put up with that son-of-a-bitch when we know he's stolen from all of us?" one would put out. Followed by, "He's a dirty, thieving bastard," and then "Lousy crooked looter," from another.

"We can string him up."

"Yeah. that would satisfy my soul, but who's going to support Gertrude and those babes?"

This usually ended the conversation but others began to think of what else they might do to vent their spleens on Willy. Many solutions from whippings, castration, leg breaking, ear removal and other divers evils were thought up. Willy felt the heat increasing.

One Thursday night he shook Gertrude hard until she roused from a deep slumber.

"Whatcha want?" she demanded, half between anger and sleepiness.

"I's decided to go. People been nice to you but they's been givin' me a rough time. Figor summun can break out. Can't take no mo chances. I'll gits my wages for the two weeks on Saday and we can leave that night. Folks won't miss us on Sunday. Be Monday 'fore they knows we's gone and they won't do nuddin then. Need to start packin' in the mornin' so we can move on."

"Why'd you wake me up for that?"

"Need for ya to be thinkin' about it. Can't haul ev'rything in that there wagon. Gotta decide what to leave. Don't wanna leave nuddin that kin sell but we can't sell it here 'cause I don't wants'em to knows we's goin'."

"You're the dumbest man. How can I be pickin' while I's asleep?"

"That's why I woke ya up, ya dumb woman. Do sum thinkin' 'fore you go back to sleep. We's only got a coupla days. And we's gonna have to have most things in the wagon by tomorrer night if we's leavin' Saday. Don't wanna mess up."

"Don't wanna go. It's been good here," Gertrude protested.

"Doncha understand? Ev'rything's about to pop loose. People startin' to make threats. Got no choice."

"The girls ain't indicated anything gonna happen to you."

"Well, I knows better and I's aleavin'. Ya can stay if ya wanna but the wagon and the kids are comin'."

"I'll think about it in the mornin'. That's 'nough time to do that. Come on to bed."

"Is ya acomin' or not?"

"Yes I'm jist ain't gonna think about what to move tonight."

CHAPTER 13

AYMOND WAS AWAKENED BY A LOUD banging on the door. He stirred sleepily and then jerked full awake. "Who the hell is it?" he yelped.

"It's Brent. Time you got your ass up. Your kindly friends are stirring and I need to check Cliff."

"Hold on," from Ay as he pulled on his pants and headed for the door. He unlocked it and pulled back the chair. Brent came in and went over to Cliff. The boy was just beginning to stir and moaned. Brent put his hand to his forehead.

"He's running a pretty high fever. Can you hear me Cliff? How you feeling?"

Cliff moaned. "I hurts right bad. Can hardly keep ma eyes open and ma head hurts sumpn awful."

"This is bad," Brent said. "Those ratskinks are on their way here and I don't think we ought to be moving the kid. I think they know where you are and they'll be back to complete the job and start one on you. And there ain't no law in this town either. I'd like to help out but I'm not much on gun slinging and fighting's not down my line. I've shot at a few Indians and tried a rifle shot at a running bank robber once, but I don't even tote a gun. Got one at home for emergencies, but I'll have to live around here for a while and I can't have them on me all the time so we're going to have to think of something to get y'all out of sight."

"Don't worry about me. I'm used to tight situations. I can handle those bullies." Ay picked up his rifle from the corner, worked the lever to inject a shell into the chamber, put it back, pulled on his shirt, buckled his gun belt, drew the revolver, checked the cylinder of the Russian Smith and Wesson, replaced it in the holster, took his converted Colt Dragoon and accessories from the saddle bag, inspected the cylinder and the spare ones, putting the extras in his two capacious vest pockets. A casual observer would not be aware of them. Ay then stuck the gun into the back of his belt and covered it with his coat. "I'm going to let the livery man know we can't leave today. I'll be right back and we'll lock the door. If they don't know whether I'm in here or not, they may be a little hesitant in trying to break open the door. Be right back."

"I'll stay here and make noises until you return. It's the least I can do considering the circumstances."

"Thanks, Brent. I won't be long. Lock the door after me." Ay looked out into the corridor and quickly and quietly slipped out the back way. Brent, as quietly, closed and locked the door.

Ay hurried behind the buildings, went down the space between two wood structures and looked carefully onto the main street. With no one in sight, he crossed quickly and headed for the stable. The big front doors were open and he went right in. A wagon was there with a small, wiry horse in harness. The liveryman, Joe Hughes, looked up.

"Got it all ready for you. That palfrey don't look like much but it's stout and mean. Really tough. She'll get you where you're going."

"Thanks old fellow, but I won't be using it today. The kid ain't up to traveling. I just popped over to let you know. Expecting a little trouble from Jake Hudson's crowd so I can't stay."

"You'll git a lot more than a little trouble from those onery cayutes. They're plum mean. Good luck to ye." Ay took off for the saloon at a brisk pace. He was crossing the street when three men appeared from behind the general store and headed for the saloon.

"Hey, you!" one of them yelled. "Hold up."

Aymond walked on determinedly, mounted the boardwalk, pushed the batwings aside and strode across the room. He was surprised to see the poker players still at it. "My God," he thought, "They must never sleep." He entered the hallway and tapped on the door. "I'm back Brent." The key turned and the door opened. Ay entered hastily and shut it behind him. "They're out there. Be here any second." He scooped up his rifle and went back out the door. You'd better scoot now, Brent. Thanks for watching out for Cliff. Take care." Ay locked the door behind them and handed the key to Brent.

"I'll be damned if I leave. Even if I am neutral I'm going to hang around and watch this. You may need my services."

"Don't expect so, Brent. But keep out of the line of fire."

"You're going to take on them hombres all by yourself? You've got to be good—or crazy!"

Ay grinned. "Hang onto the key and keep out of the line of fire, Brent."

— — —

The three walked aggressively and purposely down the street led by Josh Hicks, Jake's sidekick. Josh was big. About six, three, tall and over two hundred and sixty pounds. At one time he had been all muscle and somewhat lighter but plenty of beer, beans, steaks and whisky had fattened him. There was a definite paunch and he did not move as fast as he had when he was younger. But he had no worries. His reputation from earlier years and his size always protected him. Men gave him a clear berth. He was not the sharpest thinker in the world and had made out much better since tying up with Jake. It was Jake, the sly one, who planned the stage coach robberies, and bank busts. Money had been more plentiful for all three of them since joining forces with Jake. They had doubled as gun fighters for ranch owners, stage lines and mine owners. It gave them a false patina of lawfulness. While regular cowhands were drawing down thirty dollars a month, a gunslinger collected from forty-five to sixty. A real good man with a gun could get eighty-five to a hundred with special bonuses. Jake made top dollar while Josh was able to get a little more than the other two.

None of the four was known for his fast draw or accuracy but they did have a reputation for getting the job done. Bushwhacking and ambushes were their favorite mode of operation but they also gloried in corralling single or double cowhands and doing them in with sheer numbers. They were cagey enough not to take on even odds. Now their wrath flowed because of the injury to their money making leader. Their anger increased when Aymond ignored them.

The group came slowly up to the batwings while muttering how they were going to Bar-B-Que two young cubs. They looked inside cautiously as was their custom. They took no unnecessary chances which is why they had been around for a while. They could see Ay at the bar with his coat on the bartop, yet could not see the rifle underneath. They stepped inside and stopped, slowly separating. Mac, the bartender, still back with the card players, had not seen Ay put the gun on the bar and was without knowledge to warn the threesome. He rather hoped they would teach that young rascal a lesson.

Aymond turned and said, "I'd like a quick one, please Mac."

"Be right there." He slowly rose and headed toward the front while watching Jake's bunch.

Josh approached Aymond and growled, "Didn't you hear me calling you out there, you little tinhorn?"

"Were you calling me?" Ay replied. He slid his hand under the slicker.

"Yeah, and I'm goin' to teach you to have some respect for your betters. Now kneel down."

Ay raised the gun until Josh could see the muzzle almost in his face. "Tell your friends to have a seat at the table by the door." Josh took a half step back and realized he was caught. Any move to go for his gun could mean instant extinction.

"Hank, you and Mo sit down over there at the door."

"What the hell?" from Hank. They could not see the gun hidden by Josh's body.

"Sit down, dam'it. I said sit down." Josh had seen Aymond's eyes contracting. He wanted no open confrontation. Hank and Mo sat down. They were used to obeying orders barked by Jake and Josh.

Brent watched with disbelief, then realized where the rifle was.

Ay said to the card players and Brent, "I don't want to cause any inconvenience for you gentlemen but could I depend on you to tend to the guns while I take care of an unfinished job?"

"What are you talking about?" one of the players inquired.

"This misguided lout has been trying to run over defenseless youngsters and needs to be taught a lesson. The one given his crony didn't sink home so the time has come to give him his individual instruction. He needs to absorb some facts and a thorough beating comparable to the one administered to Cliff in there should work. I, of course, do not expect you gentlemen to join in, but only to maintain neutrality and keep those other two louts from joining in. You'll do us all a favor." Ay figured he could count on Brent and with the others in agreement he would have his backside protected. "Don't you agree—by the way what is your name? I'm aware of Jake's."

"It's Josh Hinks. Are you talking about a fist fight between you and me, no holds barred?" He could not believe his luck.

"Sure am," Ay agreed.

"Great. You fellas do like he says and watch out for any interference." Josh was thinking, "How lucky! I'll stomp him to a mushball. It'll jest take a minit or two. This little pimple thinks he can fight me." Josh was convinced of his coming victory by his past wins and his much greater height, reach and weight. "Hank, you and Mo give your guns to those guys and here's mine. He unbuckled his belt and careful not to get his hands near the pistol, took them to the back and came back taking off his coat and shirt.

Hank and Mo had surrendered their arms and the others seemed content to have Brent gather them in. Ay took off his coat, being careful to keep the Colt hidden under it and put in on the bar and then picked up the slicker with the Winchester and handed them over to Brent. Taking off his belt, he handed it to Brent also. Going back to the front, he removed his vest, placing it by the coat on the bar. His reloads would be at hand. Then taking off his shirt, he turned to face Josh.

"Y'all can't fight in here," Mac yelled. "You'll tear up the place."

"You've got a point," Ay agreed, being glad to go outside where Josh could not use chairs or bottles. Even though Ay had sized up the situation carefully and knew Josh was not fast and could not exert himself too long, he did not want a freak injury from some broken chair leg or cuts from a jagged bottle half. With bare hands he could control the outcome. Ay was in the very best physical condition. His muscles were tight and tough and he had done all sorts of fighting from Indian knife combats to wrestling and English style boxing. A Japanese friend at the University of Virginia had even taught him some strange Oriental methods. Aymond felt well prepared. Josh's sheer bulk did not dismay him.

Josh did not like the idea of going outside. Having already spotted a couple of bottles he could use, he had also eyeballed several available chairs. He even had considered the use of the table by the door now that his friends had settled in the back, but he could think of no good reason for staying inside. "All right," he assented.

Ay strode out the door with Josh right behind. Hank and Mo looked at their guns and followed. Brent allowed the others to go out and then gathered up the guns, went back to the storage room and locked them in with Cliff, but kept Ay's Russian stashed behind him in his belt. Feeling well prepared for anything, he followed the others outside.

Ay and Josh were facing each other. Josh swung a big roundhouse which Ay easily dodged and then buried his fist in the big man's gut. Josh was unprepared, the air went out of him and he collapsed on the ground. Ay stepped back, but Josh was surprisingly quick back on his feet though breathing too rapidly. Rushing at Ay and succeeding in getting a bear hug around his chest Josh squeezed hard until Ay could feel the essence going out and struggled fruitlessly with his arms. Desperate, he realized he could not break the hold. Then, in a final effort, he brought his hands up, opened them and clapped the palms over Josh's ears with a resounding bang. The shock to his ear drums forced him to let go.

"Why don't you fight like a man?" he growled and charged. Ay stepped aside and threw another solid punch to the stomach. Josh was better prepared for this one and only grunted. He took another swing at Ay which Ay ducked and threw a hard left to the face. Josh's nose broke and blood cascaded down his lips. He reached up and wiped it away and came lunging in, keeping his punch low. Ay stepped aside, instead of under, and planted another solid left to the face, which closed one of Josh's eyes. Josh turned and realized he was sweating heavily. He was beginning to get worried. This was not turning out like he had figured. His face and nose were hurting and he was beginning to have trouble breathing. He had to do something.

He started his charge again and instead of swinging with just one hand started the left slightly after he had launched the right. Ay ducked avoiding the right but was caught solidly on the side of the head by the left. Ay went down instantly, as if he were poleaxed. He shook his head to clear it when Josh landed his heavy boot on the same side of his head. Ay rolled away and felt fear spreading through him. "My God, he almost got me. I've got to be careful."

Josh came charging for another kick. Ay pulled back, barely avoiding contact, and then reached up and grabbed the leg as it went by over his head. Ay twisted hard and Josh went down. Ay regained his feet and shook his head to clear it. Josh clambered up and headed in again. He managed to catch Ay again, this time in a bearhug that contained his arms. Ay struggled to get his arms free but Josh was unrelenting. Utilizing his great weight he pushed Ay back until he was bending backward over a horsetrough. Josh was intent on bending him and breaking his back by his superior weight. Ay was desperate and kicked out at Josh's shin with all the force he could muster. He was lucky again and the blow ended the hold.

Josh yelled and bent to rub his shin when Ay hit him in the back of the neck with the edge of his hand and drove his face down into the gravel. Josh roared and came up with both arms pumping. Ay could read the telegraph well and retreated. Josh came on but with his guard lower. Ay connected with his face again in a devastating blow. Blood was going everywhere. The nose looked loose and the forehead and lips were split and torn. Josh came roaring in one more time and Ay punished his face again with three more blows and then an uppercut. Josh sank to the ground whimpering.

"You brutes never learn. A beating can hurt. How much more do you want?"

"Pleeze, not no mo'. That's nuff," Josh begged in a low voice.

"Get out of here. You and your friends can come back for you guns tomorrow."

Hank and Mo helped Josh up and started down the street. "That lousy bastard." Josh was breathing hard and barely able to talk. "He didn't fight fair. Did ya see how he slapped my ears. Like a kid fighting. I'll git'm. I'll git'm," he mumbled.

"Josh, I've got a rifle up in the room. We can go up there and get him. My stash gun is here but there're too many of them now. We can get him with the rifle from our room."

"That sounds good. Ooooh! My face is killing me. Lend me your kerchief, Mo. I need to get the blood off. I kin barely see."

But Josh, it's a new one. It'll get all bloody."

"Get the damn thing off. I'm hurtin', I tell ya."

Mo handed it over and Josh pushed it gently to his mangled face.

"Let's get on up to the room so Hank can take care of that sneaking kid." Josh wanted vengeance and did not intend to stop until his soul was satisfied.

CHAPTER 14

CAIN'S WAGON LUMBERED ON TOWARD
the blind canyon. Willy had left early Saturday night and headed
south to leave a false trail. Coming to his first stream he headed
down river until he found a gravelly bank and exited northward but
not before smoothing out the small stones. Come the next rain, he
figured and there would be no trace. He continued on with an easy
mind.

The wagon was loaded with piled funiture, foodstuffs, trading
items along with Gertrude and the two youngsters. He had long ago
gotten rid of the horses he had acquired before getting to Boonetown.
Except for the two children, he had cut all connections with the
past. He wanted to have nothing which could point him out as a
thief of any kind. Although not a great intellect, he had basic cunning.

Arriving at the canyon entrance he unhitched the nag and set it
out to graze. Leaving the children in the wagon, he and Gertrude
set out to find the penned horses. They turned out to be skittish and
kept retreating to the back of the canyon. By staying between them
and the exit, the pair finally got a rope on one. Gertrude was im-
pressed with the quality of the horseflesh. Months of leisure and
good grass and water had filled and sleeked them out.

It did not take Willy long to get a bridle and saddle on the jet
black stallion. Willy had figured him for the toughest one to rebreak
but he had adapted easily and Willy used him to gather up the other
two. Leading them back to the concealed wagon he had hidden
months ago, he staked them out and uncovered the wagon.

With Gertrude's help he put the wheels back on, a slow operation requiring the cutting of several trees used as levers and fulcrums. At the end of three days he was ready to move out. The children had enjoyed a holiday. With no one around they had been allowed the freedom of the canyon. Willy knew they could not run off and so had just turned them loose with the admonition not to stray too far or the wolves might get them. They found the new empty wagon a playground for more fun. As they left the canyon, with Gertrude driving them and Willy in the laden one, their time off continued.

Willy then headed for his hideyhole having told Gertrude that they had other assets.

"We'll have to sell most of the stuff, Gertie. I don't wanna have it around."

Having guessed the reason, she grunted and changed the subject. "Where you planning on lightin'?"

"There's a small place called Tater Patch up the road a spell where I hear they can use a second bartender. I'll gotta be careful and not be caught in any shenanigans there. We'll have to show up like a down and out fam'ly and start from scratch. My operations are gonna hav'ta be a long way off. If we can't work it there, we'll push on. It means we gonna hav'ta sell mossa things before we gits there. I sho don't want nuddin hanging around when we're settled down.

CHAPTER 15

"WELL, THAT WAS SOME SHOW," BRENT grinned. "I guess I've another new patient now. Their guns are locked in the room. Here's the key. Don't imagine you'll be bothered for a while. I'm going over and doctor on Josh now. Be back for a drink. Save me half the bottle. You might need some medical ministrations too. Save me some libations." Brent left for the space over the general store that was Jake's main quarters. The players went back to their game after slapping Ay on the back and telling him what a great job he had done. They were careful to wait until Josh and his companions were well gone before doing it.

"Careful young fellow," said one. "Those hard noses aren't through. They'll be after you with a gun now. That fight was a good one but it didn't end anything. They'll still be after you and no warnings either. Could be lead in the back from that crowd. They like to push their weight around."

"Come on deal," insisted another. "Leave the preaching for the Bible pushers."

"Thank you for your solicitous words, my friends. I'll be alert," said Ay half facetiously.

The game resumed.

Ay went to the back room, locked the door and pushed a chair under the handle, shucked his boots and though hurting all over and with additional sharp pain in a few places, felt secure, and joined Cliff in raucous snoring.

— — —

The knocking came loud and insistent. "Open up you deadhead!

It's me, Brent. Get this door open. I'm thirsty."

Aymond forced his eyes open although he felt drugged. But he sat up and, instantly, was back in control. He had not been sleeping warily as he usually did but had been totally relaxed. His aches came back rapidly and he grunted slightly as a knife-like pain slashed across his ribs. He swung his feet to the floor and forced himself upright, moved to the door, flipped back the chair and turned the key. "Come on in you killsleep. I was a helluva lot more comfortable until you woke me up."

"'S t'bad my friend. I'm in bad need of that drink. You ruint my night with what you did to Josh. He's going to be like Jake and take a while to come round. Where's the bottle?"

"I don't know. It's around somewhere. I just piled in after I got my boots off." Ay rummaged around his coat and came up with the lost container. "Voila, here's your precious liquor, and over half a bottle left."

"Great." Brent took a healthy slug and sat nursing the bottle between his knees. He grunted several times, belched loudly and downed another slug. "Need to talk to you, son. Those hard heads can't take a licking. They're still after blood and this time I've a feeling they'll dry gulch you. There's been rumors of them being responsible for some back shooting around here but nobody's been able to pin anything on them but most of us know them for what they are. Been some talk of necktie parties but most of the folks around here don't want to take on all four of 'em at the same time. So I'm giving you the straight word. Watch your backside!"

"Figured as much. I'm usually careful about that sort of thing anyway, but now I'll just screw myself down tighter and be twice as watchful."

"How's Cliff doing?"

"Don't know. I've been cutting those logs pretty heavy. Check him out yourself. You're the doctor."

"Let's just let him sleep. It's good for him and waking him up 'snot going to help anything at the moment. Want some of this bottle?"

"No thanks. I'm feeling more like breakfast. What time is it?"

Brent took out a huge, yellow cased watch, flipped up the lid and entoned, "Six O'clock at the sound of the chimes. Dong, dong dong," he went with loud laughter. Cliff stirred, and then turned over. "Sorry, forgot about our hurting friend," he said more quietly.

"What about me, you no good codger? Here I am black and purple all over and feeling like the fiend has his pitchfork in me in twenty places and all you're interested in is the no good Josh and that damn bottle."

"Don't speak of man's boon companion and resuscitator of broken bodies in such a snide way, my friend. This is nectar for the gods and a tired man's balm. Speak not of it harshly."

"I can see it's having its effect on you."

"Oh, my friend, be not so hard on a working medico who labored hard during the hours of the darkness while you slumbered away the night. My bones do rebel against such continued drudgery."

"Enough's enough," Ay laughed. "Bring your solicitous liquid, while I search for some morning grub. I can't remember awaking to the company of an inebriated man before." He pulled on his boots and headed for the door. "Come on."

"'Beware your backside!' as the witches said to Macbeth."

"It's well buckled on," laughed Ay again while stroking his pistol butt. "Come on." Ay peered up and down the hall, beckoned Brent through, then shut and locked the door. The card players were still at the table though one was asleep with his head on the table. The others were beginning to appear winded.

"About done I'd say," allowed Brent. "Where in the hell is the barkeep? He could scrounge up some breakfast. Think I'll have some too, but it's a shame to end such a mellow glow."

"Bartender," yelled Ay. "You've got some hungry men out here. Get a leg on." The bartender finally came down the hall stuffing in his shirttail and with his suspenders dragging behind.

"I'm coming, I'm coming. Just hold on."

"Get some eggs, bacon and pan fried bread out here and some strong black coffee right now," Aymond ordered.

"Not no coffee right now. I've got to start the fire. Got some cold dregs from yestiddy if you'se wants it." McKenzie was decidedly amicable.

"Yeah, that'll do for now. Bring it in."

"Not me, I'll wait," declared Brent. "I'll just have some more of this friendly bottle." He suited action to the word with another healthy blast. "How are you doing? Looks to me I can see some blue spots in places and there's dried blood on the back of your neck."

"Now you get concerned after taking care of bully boy and neglecting the victor. It's what I was trying to tell you when you started on your dissertation on the amber liquid. Just ignoring me and helping the enemy."

"He needed it more than you did. Are you doing all right?"

"I hurt like hell all over. But I don't think there're any broken bones."

"I'll check you when we finish breakfast. No question of your survival."

Mac finally made it in with hot coffee. After several quick swallows, Ay added, "At least he makes good coffee. Damn hot and pitch strong." Breakfast soon arrived and Ay showed his beating had not slowed his appetite.

"Well, now that you've surrounded your groceries, we can go get a look at Cliff," said Brent standing up.

Ay was careful to check completely around before he rose and followed Brent. He checked the corridor and then approached the door. Since he could hear no sounds from inside, he opened the door with a quick push but nothing was awry. Cliff was gently snoring.

"I hate to wake him but I need to get some sack time myself. I'm getting really bushed." Brent touched Cliff on the shoulder and the boy groaned as he opened his eyes. "Sorry to bother you fellow, but I need to check you out before I leave. You've been sleeping well. How do you feel?"

"My God, doc, it hurts."

"Whereabouts?"

"All over."

"Ay, get on the other side and let's get him sitting up. This is going to hurt a lot more but we need to check these wrappings." Ay and Brent got him to a sitting position. "No signs of bleeding and I think his fever's down some. Definite signs of mending. You ought to be able to start for Lizard Sands by the day after tomorrow."

"I can make it now, doc."

"No you can't. Too much jostling too soon can break those things open and you'll be bleeding again. Got to give it a couple of days."

"We'll wait, Brent," and turning, "Take it easy Cliff. No big rush. You just eat and rest and we'll pull out Thursday."

"No problem, Ay. I'll stay."

"No real choice, son." Ay grinned inwardly at his assumed paternal attitude toward Cliff who was only marginally younger. Ay had been grown long before his time.

CHAPTER 16

JAKE HUDSON WAS FUMING. "THAT NO good, stinking, green turd-head is still in town. Here I've got a crushed ankle and likely to be hobbling with a limp from now on and that son-of-a-bitch thinks he can stay here and taunt me."

"It's not that," Josh replied. "The kid's too hurt to travel. Brent told me."

"Yeh, and it looks like that Brent's gittin' too cuddly close to'em for my thinkin'. Is he sellin' us down the river?"

"Ah, come off it Jake. He's been taking good care of us. Where'd we be if he hadn't helped out?"

"Probably laughin' at us behind his back. I don't trust'm. We need to do summin to take out turdhead. Hank, you're good with a rifle. Get to one of them second floor winders that o'erlook that there saloon door and we'll take him out when he sticks his nose in the street. Mo, you get you ass down on the porch in a chair and when he comes out make him go for his gun. Everybody'll think you outdrawed him. In the meantime Hank, don't let him get his gun out and get him good the first time. Mo, you can finish him off and it'll look good. Now get to it."

Mo shuffled out and Hank picked up his rifle and followed. Mo went out into the street and looked up at the front windows. Hank appeared at the one closest to the saloon and Mo waved.

"That stupid son-of-a-bitch. What does he think he'd doin'? Givin' me away?" Hank muttered to himself. Mo went back to the porch, settled on the chair, moved his gun so he could get to it easily and undid the strap. He eased the gun out several times and yanked it once. Satisfied he settled back in the chair and began his vigil.

Time passed and no Aymond appeared. Mo was getting impatient. "Where's that son-of-a-bitch," he thought. "What was it Jake called him? Yeh, turd-head, That's what he is, a turd-head. Come on out you turd-head. I won't need no help from Hank. I'll get you myself." He tipped the chair back and stretched out his legs. More time passed and still no Aymond. Mo was getting restless. He got up, stretched, yawned, and settled down again. He was beginning to get hungry.

What Mo did not know was that Brent had looked out over the batwings and saw him leaning back in the chair watching the saloon front. Brent went back to the storage room, knocked and said,

"It's me, Brent. Let me back in."

"What is it?" replied Ay opening the door.

"I think they're laying for you. Mo's on the porch across the street keeping an eye on this place."

"I'll take a look," Ay said as he locked the door behind him. He walked down the hall and toward a front window, stopping about ten feet back. He moved sideways until he spotted Mo. "He's sure watching. He looks right nervous to me."

Mo was still wiggling restlessly. He was really hungry now and getting mad because the turdhead had not come out.

"I think I'll let him stew some more," Ay allowed. "I can use some extra shuteye. I'm going back and take a nap. I'd go out right careful, if I were you Brent. He's looking real nervous and might not be too attentive."

"Think you're right. Mo's not too discerning. I'll just leave the back way. Just as well not take chances. See you later, Ay."

— — —

Mo was getting jumpy. He would spring up when he thought he spotted something, take out his pistol and spin the cylinder, then sit back down and immediately jump up again. He wanted to walk out in the street and wave at Hank but realized this was not a good idea. He squirmed and noted that his stomach was hollering at him. He needed something to eat bad. He squirmed some more and then made up his mind. He would go upstairs and get Hank and go get something to eat. He leaped up and ran inside, went to the steps and started up while bellowing. "Hank, Hank."

"What the hell's the matter with you?" Hank replied.

"I'm hungry."

"Oh crap! I'm hungry; I'm hungry," he mimicked. "You sorry bastard. Here we've got a job to do and all you can think about is 'I'm hungry.' You no good lousy bastard. Don't you know we've got a job to do and all you think about is missin' a meal."

"But Hank, I'm real hungry."

"Oh, damnit,all right. Guess ussons can catch'im later, He sho ain't done nuddin all mornin'". They went back to Jake's quarters and Hank brought him up to date.

"Go eat but just get back on the job pronto,"

— — —

"I think they've gone. Probably to get something to eat. Now's a good time to check the horses," said Brent peering out the saloon window.

"I'll go," replied Ay. "Probably come back the back way." He slipped out the swinging gates and headed for the livery stable. The big double doors were open and Joe Hughes was moving hay with a pitchfork. "How's everything, Joe?"

"All right, young fellow. When you gonna be ready to leave?"

"Probably Thursday. Cliff's still hurting and Brent feels he needs a little more time."

"Heard you stomped on Josh. Ain't gonna do you any good. They'll back shoot you now."

"Yeah, that's what Brent said, but I'm watching my backside. 'Preciate your letting me know if you hear or see anything."

"Have to be careful with them hoodlums, but I'll holler if I can."

"Do appreciate it. Thanks." Ay looked out and then ducked between the two buildings, checked the main street and slipped across and then into the back door of the saloon. Brent let him in.

"How're the horses?"

"Fine. Joe's ready whenever we can move Cliff. I told him we're shooting for Thursday. Mo wasn't there when I sneaked across. Wonder what's going on?"

"He'll be back. They're not that innovative. Just wait. He'll plop into that same chair and I've got a good feeling Hank's going to be at that upstairs window."

"Well, I can't stay holed up forever. I'll check'em out sooner or later, but there's no use your hanging around and being in the line of fire. You've been a real help, but it looks like this is my show now."

"Kinda hate to leave you by yourself. I'll miss the exciting part. Feel you can handle it but be very careful. Don't take anything for granted. They're capable of almost any vile act, so stay awake."

"Thanks, Brent. I'll watch."

Brent departed by the back door.

——— ——— ———

Mo settled back in his chair and rubbed his tight stomach, The chow had been good. He loved a loin steak with beans and potatoes and had taken more than his share. He was ready for Aymond now. "Bring on that turd-head," he thought. "I'll get'm now." He swayed back easily, stretched out his legs and relaxed.

MacKenzie had taken a break, left his bar, and strolled down Main Street to the see the Postmistress at Hastings Emporium. Pausing on his return, Mac had let Mo and Hank know that Aymond was still inside the saloon.

Aymond watched him from several yards back from the window. He heard the bartender coming in the back way and figured correctly that Mac had been reporting to the enemy.

"Get your ass back to your quarters. And if I see you again before this is over, I'm shoving you out in front of me with my coat and hat on. Now think it over."

Mac digested the information quickly and scurried back to his rooms.

"Don't come out," Ay yelled after him. He looked back across the street where he could tell Mo was having a tough time keeping his eyes open. They would shut, he would slump over and jerk back up, look around and nod again. Ay could see the glint of of the rifle's barrel in the window above and watched as the barrel slowly lowered to the window sill. He had a feeling that Hank was getting drowsy too. "Well, if I'm going, I don't think I can get a better situation." He waited until two women came out of the general store turned left and strolled conversing toward the residential area. Mo opened his eyes, looked around and nodded again with his chin on his chest. When the two women were safely out of the way, Ay loosened the strap on his gun, pulled it a few times, then checked the situation across the street and moved rapidly through the batwings.

He was almost to the middle of the street when Mo looked up and yelled, jumping to his feet and slapping for his gun. Looking up, Ay saw the rifle lift, pulled and fired at the window and immediately got off a second shot at Mo, who had just gotten his gun from his holster and was swinging it toward Aymond. Aymond's second shot got the trigger guard and the gun and Mo's trigger finger went smashing against the wall. Mo started yelling and jumping up and down while the rifle from above slid down the porch roof and into the street. Aymond scooped it up as he moved in. Mo presented no more threats for the moment and Aymond went inside and cautiously up the steps. Hank was slumped against a wall with blood gushing from his front. He looked up at Aymond, tried to say something before falling. Aymond could tell he was dead. He went back down to Mo who was still jumping around and screaming, waving his hand and yelling.

Jake came hobbling up shouting, "You shot these men without warning. You're a murderer and a coward."

"How did you know there are men? There's only one in sight," said Aymond turning with his gun still in his hand.

"I saw you shoot up at that window and come down with that rifle in your hand. You're a murderer."

"Come off it, Jake. We all saw what happened. Mo drew on him and Hank was trying to bushwhack him from the window. That rifle came off the roof." This from Joe Hughes who had come up behind Jake.

"That's right," from one of the two women who came hurrying back. That gun fell off the roof and he picked it up before he went inside.

Jake turned away muttering. "Come on Mo," he called back. Down to half-hollers, Mo followed him. Aymond walked over and picked up Mo's revolver and looked at the bloody, smashed finger in disgust and turning, walked back into the saloon.

CHAPTER 17

BRENT WAS CHECKING THE WRAPPING ON Mo's hand. "It's quite bloody. I'll have to change it." Mo moaned as the bandage was unwound. The finger stub was red, raw and ugly. "I don't think you'll get gangrene. But you'll need more iodine."

"No!" yelled Mo in violent protest.

"Yes," said Brent pouring it on. Mo yelled louder.

"I'll get that bastard. I'll get that turd-head if it's the last thing I ever do," snarled Jake.

"It probably will be," inserted Brent.

"Will be what?" snarled Mo.

"Won't you dumb, misbegotten dolts ever learn? Three of you crippled and the fourth up on Boot Hill. You amateurs are no match for a professional. You had better move on before he decides you're a menace to the decent folk. He might decide to take your legs off next and maybe blind you."

"My God, he wouldn't do that would he?"

"Wouldn't be surprised if you got him riled again. You fellows sure are slow learners. Even the town people have decided it's time for you to move on. They can tell when the wolves' teeth have been pulled. I'd suggest you quietly leave while you can. I heard talk of a necktie party. Some of these people remember a few things. Wouldn't want to have to make boxes for three more of you and you owe me six dollars for Hank."

"Why should I pay you for Hank?" Jake snorted.

"He worked for you and ended up where he did because he worked for you. Only right. And besides you don't need any more enemies, especially while two of you still need a lot more nursing."

Oh, I didn't think o'that. I ketch on. Here's your six bucks. But I'll remember it."

"See that you do in more ways than one." And after digging in his bag, "Here's some laudanum, Mo. It'll ease the pain." He poured some into a spoon and pushed it down. "You're going to have to learn to use a gun with your left hand. It's going to be too awkward without that finger. Try it if you want to but I suggest you start practicing with your left. You may never be good with it but it's better than nothing."

"Ah, shit," from Mo.

"I'd leave today. A word to the wise. Here, Mo," handing him the bottle. "Half a spoonful when it hurts too bad to stand. Don't use it right up because you won't be able to get any more too easy. That stuff is not kept by just anybody. Josh, here's some iodine for you and Mo. Use it as long as you've got open sores." Handing over another small bottle,he added, "Now I'd get gone if I were y'all."

"Damn, it's going to be hard to travel like this,' Jake complained loudly.

"Beats ending up in boxes," Brent rejoined.

— — —

Three bedraggled men gathered their horses from Joe Hughes and started south. They knew Aymond was going north.

"Good riddance," sighed Joe.

CHAPTER 18

AYMOND WAS DRIVING THE SMALL BUCK-
board with Clifford Jones tucked in the back, well doused with
whisky. Joshua and Jericho with Cliff's bedraggled mare were tied
on behind and the going was slow . Cliff jerked and sat upright,
suddenly giving an intense moan.

"You all right?"

"Ooohhh," groaned Cliff.

"How you feeling, Cliff?"

"Purrrrty good, Aymond."

But Aymond could tell the boy was concealing the truth. "Well I
think Brent was a little unhappy we left when we did, but I'd been
hanging around Potato Patch too long. Dad's going to be worried
about me even tho he knows I can take care of myself. Brent promised to come up to Lizard Sands for a visit when he could and insisted we come back to Potato Patch the next time Dad goes. Like to
see him but don't think much of taking up with McKenzie again.
Was really pleased to hear those three rattlesnakes left heading
south. I've had enough of their venom. You get back to sleep. Better
for you and we've got miles to go. No use your being conscious of
them. Stretch on back out."

Aymond wondered what Cain was doing.

— — —

Cain was moving north. Finding a broken down wagon train,
which had barely survived a Commanche attack, he sold off almost
everything. The wagon-trainers still had gold coins but were ecstatic
over healthy horses, a solid wagon, and a trove of usable items in-

cluding a small barrel. Willy ended up with a goodly number of the gold coins.

"Well Gertie, ya gotta grant me, I know howta trade."

"Sho do, Willy, but you shoulda kept two good horses and let them have that plug we left Boonetown with."

"Couldn't git real money for that one Gertie, We'll do fine with one good horse and one so-so one."

"'Tain't so-so. It's a lousy no good."

"Qitcha bitchin', Gertie. We done all right."

— — —

At that moment Joe Hughes and Brent Stephenson were addressing McKenzie. "Mac, while Jake and his crew were riding high we had to put up with your shenanigans. But now they're gone and we're going to give you one friendly word of warning. We don't care who backs your play from now on. If you don't behave in a neighborly way to people here and regular folks passing through, we just might give you the Mo treatment and send you on minus two trigger fingers. Do you understand? It's hard to realize that you're alive now. The poker gang tells us you pointed a shotgun at Aymond and pulled both triggers. Yeah, mighty hard to realize you're still living. But don't count on such luck next time. I hope we are understood?"

"Yeah."

"We mean it Mac. Do you understand?"

"I understand."

"All right. Now let's get back on a level plane. Just run a first class bar and everything'll be fine."

— — —

Aynond could see the round room with the widow's walk atop it long before there was a hint of a town over the next rise. It had been almost three years since he had been up there with Doc Bearman. The turnoff to Doc's place was still the same. He wondered about Ahgy, Doc's Man Friday He now wondered about Doc himself. There had been no bad reports in Potato Patch. In fact there had been no reports of any kind and he became uneasy. Recalling Mandy's old saying that bad news traveled fast, he relaxed. If something had happened to Doc the news would have come down. The fact that the passers-through had no news of moment meant all was well. As he reached the crest of the hill he pulled up old Lizzy and looked down on Lizard Sands. It had grown with several dozen more houses. Main street had been extended two blocks and there were more businesses in the buildings. Lizard Sands could rightly be called a town although it was no city. Houses had even grown up beyond Doc's which for so long had been outside the edge of town.

It had been from atop Doc's house that the Comanches had been spotted charging in and who were stopped decisively after only one charge down Main Street. That attack, about ten years ago, was the last one except for horses stolen and raids on outlying ranches. Indians did not bother towns now but they could be hell on travelers and undermanned farms and ranches.

Miners were particularly vulnerable but tended to stay in groups for self protection. Since the size of a claim was limited, they welcomed other miners to their sites, so long as the newcomers stayed off the settled workings. It was the loner who was most vulnerable. Some of these were wise in Indian ways and, with proper precautions, survived to old age.

Indians were retreating to the mountains and other wild areas, while others were going more and more into the Nations and other reservations but could not be counted on to stay there. The ingrained customs of raiding and taking of enemy horses and livestock were too dominant. The plains tribes were the worst: the Commanches, Sioux, Kiowas, Cheyenne, Blackfeet and the mountain Apaches. Aymond had been careful and lucky. Though he has seen Indian signs on many occasions he had avoided any face to face contact which could have had painful consequences. His last sighting had been far south of Potato Patch.

Aymond wondered what Little Jenny and Mary Matlock were doing. He was beginning to have trouble recalling their faces. He knew they were pretty and lively. Jenny was the sassy one and Mary shy or was it the other way around? He had been there such a short time and they certainly were nice: prettier than most girls back east. He would have to go back and visit.

He wondered if George Allen, the other youngster he was helping, had made it from the Matlocks to Lizard Sands. George had been naturally bitter and eager to get his mother's killer, but had been held back by his physical condition. It might have been better to have waited until George was well before moving on from the Matlocks, since he had not caught Cain. Second guessing was no good. Make up your mind and do it. No use worrying about taking wrong turns—and they may not have been wrong. Finally his thoughts came back to Cain and he wondered where he was and what had happened to him. In Lizard Sands he could receive reports of troubles which might give him a lead. It had the telegraph although no railway yet. His thoughts drifted back to the Matlock girls again. He grinned. "Sure have to go back there soon." Starting back up, he headed down the hill.

"We're home Cliff. I've seen the whole town. We should be at Dad's in about fifteen minutes."

"Really glad to be here, Ay," added Cliff, rubbing a sore spot.

CHAPTER 19

CAIN, BEING ALSO LINDSEY BENEDICT,
alias Willy Sharpe, turned his horse and shouted, "Keep up, Gertie.
We'll have to camp out again tonight if we don't reach Potato Patch
in another hour or two." Willy was off on his distances; Potato Patch
was still over two days away.

"This old nag won't go no faster. I told you to keep a proper
horse but you don't pay no 'tention. Who's those fellas coming yon-
der?" Gertrude had spotted Jake and his other two cripples. "They
sho look right poorly."

"Don't look too dangerous, but keep that shotgun under your
skirt. Ne'er know."

"Howdy friends," said Willy looking them over carefully and deciding there was not much worth the effort of taking.

"Howdy there," answered Jake also deciding against any violence in realizing his group was not much force and Willy and
Gertrude looked capable of taking care of themselves. "We're on our
way to Boonetown. Have you come from that way?"

"Yep," replied Willy.

"How much farther is it along?"

"Oh, three or four days, depending. We're heading for Potato
Patch."

"Just two more days, friend."

"You mean it ain't just down the way?"

"Nope, two days of good traveling."

"We sho was told wrong. My God, Gertie, we'll ne'er git there.
Any Injun activity back your way?"

"Nope. What about south?"

"Few scattered cases. Almost all on small parties, so keep a good watch out. We ain't had no problems but you never know. Sho hate it that Tater Patch is so far away but thanks anyway, friend. Come on hoss, git movin'! Come on Gertie." Willy and the wagon started up while Jake and the others continued south.

After several miles of slow going, "Ain't been nuttin' to replenish us from. Nobody movin' this way, one way or t'other," Willy complained. Sally and little Joey looked out from the wagon, too beat down to complain. Their fun days were behind them and they were penned up in the wagon with all the accumulated objects. They did not have much to look forward to. Even Gertrude had been snarling at them lately. They crawled over a trunk and table to the back of the wagon.

"Maybe we can get away in Potato Patch, Sally," Joey whispered. Sally started crying.

"Hush up back there," Gertrude shouted. "No whinin' outuv you kids now." Silence returned as Sally wiped her face with her skirt.

— — —

Aymond started the wagon down the slope toward Bearman Manor. "Hang on now, Cliff, We're just about there." He could see Mandy clipping fresh washed shirts to the clothesline. "Hey, Mandy," he yelled in an excited voice.

Mandy turned and shielded her eyes. "It's Aymond! It's Massa Aymond done come home! Oh, Dio, Dio, Aymond's back! Aymond's back!" She ran toward the wagon calling, "Aymond, Aymond." He jumped from the buckboard, and picked her up and swung her around several exuberant times.

Kissed her vigorously all over face and neck and then hugging her tight, he enthused, "Oh, Mandy, it's so good to be back and you're looking grand, really grand."

"Oh get on wi' ya," she blushed underneath her dark skin. "You knows I'm a mess from washin' and hangin' up da clothes. Always a fibbin' but in such a nice way. Come on in, boy, come on in."

"Need a little help, Mandy. Is Ahgy around?"

"I called that no good nigga and he ain't never answered."

"I've got a hurt kid in the back of the wagon and am going to need a little help moving him in."

"What's wrong with the poor fella?" asked Mandy peering over the edge of the wagon. She was help and sympathy rolled into one competent package. "Let me get that no good Diogenes." She hustled into the house.

"You're home now, Cliff. We'll have you inside in a few minutes. That was Mandy. She'll take first class care of you and won't take any sassing so watch what you say. She's a first class lady."

"I ain't goin' to say nuttin'. Don't worry."

Mandy came sailing out of the house with Diogenes in tow. Age was beginning to show on Diogenes but he still walked upright, not slumping, but not quite so agile as Mandy. His hair was white, thinning some but with a full white beard. He went directly up to Aymond and began to pump his hand. He was as glad to see Aymond as Mandy but showed it in a more restrained way.

"Oh, Ay, it sure is good to see you! My, my haven't ya grown. Taller than me now and you're starting to fill out. What a sight for sore eyes. You certainly are. It's surely is great to see you again, Ay. Youth went away; a man returns. Wait till Doc Bearman gets home. He's certain to be pleased. Well come on in; here I am carrying on as if I had no manners. Come on in and have some coffee. Mandy's got a pot on and let us look at you. It's really good you're back after so long, Didn't think you were ever coming home."

"Whoa there; hold the horses. Didn't Mandy tell you? I've got an injured lad here in the wagon and we're going to need to get him inside."

"She was so excited about you she plumb neglected to mention it or if she did, I was too excited to hear it. We'll get him right in. We'll get that light cot Doc has and the two of us should be able to tote him right in." Diogenes started off for the house with Aymond following. They were back shortly with a lightweight, folding, metal cot between them. They put it down next to the buckboard and Ay said, "How're we going to work this?"

"Put it up in the bed of the wagon and lift him in it. Mandy can help us hand him down." Diogenes was an old hand in helping Doc unload injured men. The transfer to the bed was quickly done and the three set him on the ground.

"What room can he stay in Diogenes?" I don't think it's too good an idea to take him upstairs yet."

"We can put him in the patient room next to Doc's study.

"Yes, that'll work. Let's go." Ay and Diogenes lifted the cot from head and foot, through the front door which Mandy held open and then down the hall into a small room with two other cots and placed Cliff under the window. How you feeling now, old scout?"

"I'll make it Ay, but I sure am still hurtin' some bad. Your dad sure does have a swell place."

"That he does, Cliff. That he does."

"I's'll get a little food goin'," said Mandy as she headed out and down the hall.

"You always could take care of important things," answered Aymond laughingly as he followed.

"Is there anything you need, young man?" inquired Diogenes,

"No, I'm fine. I just think I'll rest a spell."

Doc Bearman came riding up on Rastus. This mule was faster than most horses and until his and Doc's reputation got around, Doc picked up a lot of extra change betting with the unknowledgeable. Coming up quickly, he saw the extra horses and mule in the corral and came rushing into the house. "Where is that boy?" he asked excitedly.

"He's in the patient room," Mandy responded.

"He's not hurt is he?" Doc asked as he hurried through the kitchen."

"Nope, jus that young boy with'im."

"Oh, Aymond it's certainly great to see you home! What a true sight for sore eyes," accompanied by a hearty handshake and bear hug. "Who's your young friend?"

"He's a youngster I saw being worked over in Potato Patch for no reason at all. He was hurt pretty bad, but Brent Stephenson patched him up right well but said he could benefit from your ministrations."

"Yep, Brent's a good man. Does good emergency medical work

too. Well, I'll take a look at him. What's your name young man? I'm James Bearman."

"Cliff Jones, Doc."

"How're you feeling?" as he raised Cliff's wrist and started counting his pulse.

"Not too bad, but I do hurt all over, 'specially in my chest."

"Do you think you can sit up?'

"I'll try, but it sho hurts."

"Ay, get on the other side and help me pick him up," as Doc moved the cot out from the window. They set Cliff upright and Doc started unreeling the bandage. "Man you're still black." He leaned over to sniff the skin. "Doesn't seem morbid though." He nudged at the lower ribs gently.

"Ow!" yelped Cliff.

"It won't kill you. Just hang on to Aymond while I get a couple of things. He went out and returned with jars of ointment which he gently applied to Cliff's chest. "That should help as well as taking some of the sting and ache out."

"It's 'ginin' to feel better already, Doc."

"Brent set your ribs fine and you're mending nicely. Going to have some small knots but nothing to worry about or get in your way. Now let me look at you head. Hmmm, healing abrasions. The one on your cheek should heal without a scar. The one on the back of your neck will show though. It runs up into your hair. Let you hair grow long and it won't show either. Now let's check your legs. Bruises almost gone. Stitching on the back of your leg is holding well and the wound has drained fine. Should close right up with no trouble. All right on this end. Well, I can give you a good prognosis. Back together as good as new in six weeks. Getting around right well in two. How's that suit?"

"Sound's grand, Doc. Thanks so much."

"Your thanks are due Stephenson. He got you over the hump. Here Aymond, let's get him wrapped back up," bringing out new bandages.

Do you think you can get a nap now? I see Mandy's fixed you up with some hot grub."

109

"Sure, Doc. I'm still havin' a little trouble getting it down 'cause my mouth's still sore. But it was mostly soup with little bitty pieces of meat, so I got it down. Hurts to chew."

"Well, sack out and we'll check back with you later. Rest is really what you need most and they'll be no more buckboard jumping for a while. Take it easy."

Doc and Ay went out and down the hall to Doc's study where they plopped down into two easy chairs facing each other. "It's sure good to have you back, son," and with uncontained enthusiasm, "Just fine! Just fine!" sitting back with contentment evident in his whole being.

"We have so much ground to cover. Almost three years. How are you feeling?"

"Not so bad, Dad. Got some bruises and cuts in a tussle but they're almost gone."

"What's this?" said Doc, jumping up. "I didn't know you were hurt too. Let's take a look," he insisted

Oh, it's not like Cliff's. I got into a fight with one of the assailants and he got the worst of it. Nothing that shows bad on me."

"Never mind. Off with that shirt and I'll have a look."

"It's really nothing, Dad," as he removed his vest and shirt, knowing he could not argue with Doc.

"Doesn't look so bad. Did Brent help you too?"

"Sure did."

"Well he did a superb job. Couldn't have done better myself. He's sure an asset to Potato Patch. Maybe we can lure him up here. Lizard Sands could use a man like that. A lot of time we get the drifters and no goods but if Texas is going to stay a great state, we're going to have to encourage the hard workers, the good types, and honest men. Brent should be able to do better here in Lizard Sands. Which reminds me, what do you have on your mind now that you're home?"

"Well, you remember that woman killer I was after?"

"Yes."

"As you know, I lost track of him. I think he may have taken up with some woman and passes himself off as a family. But I'm not sure. The Indians could have done him in, or he could have gone to

110

Montana or California. I lean toward the last two because his modus operandi is to attack a small group and make it appear Indians did the mischief, and I'm not aware of any such lately."

"You've been too busy with your fights then. We've had news of isolated Indian raids down around Boonetown and moving this way. In fact, there was one that came on the wire this morning that was just below Potato Patch."

"He could be at it again. I certainly haven't heard that report. See if you can get any details. Maybe Brent could get a letter off to us. I've got to get that buckboard and horse back to Potato Patch. It can take a letter to Brent and he might be able to find out something. If that bastard is on the loose again he has to be stopped. He's merciless. By the way, did that other kid, George Allen, show up?"

"Sure did. Came in with a bedraggled horse about three months ago. Was about as bedraggled himself. Told me about his mother. You were certainly right about Cain. A completely merciless, no good killer. Glad you did what you did. Maybe we can do something to put an end to his machinations. We'll put our minds to it. I'm very proud of you, Ay, in the way you took right out after him. George sure wants to help. He's turned fifteen and is back in good condition. In fact, turning plump. Mandy's cooking.

"Jane's been teaching him arithmetic and a few things, and I've started him on reading," Doc continued. "He knew his ABC's but hadn't been around many books. His English is bad but seems to know his Bible pretty well. He's been charging around like a mule with dysentery trying to get at Cain but we've convinced him that just heading out without some information or plan is worse than staying here and waiting. I don't think it would hurt him to travel with you. I'm sure he can keep up and the experience will help him. He's been practicing his shooting and coming on well with a Winchester. Kinda slow with a Colt, though. He might improve with practice but he's still uncoordinated."

"Where is George? I sure would like to see him and bring him up to date."

"He's out doing a little gun practicing. I've let him see your letters. He knows about the other killing in Haley's Crossroad and even had met the lady a few times and it stirred him up more. Hard to keep him here. He's going to be a fine backup for you."

"Certainly has the motivation," Ay agreed.

CHAPTER 20

CAIN URGED HIS HORSE TO A FASTER PACE, having spotted a man leading a pack horse over in a clump of trees just on the horizon. Lindsey Benedict was eager to check him out and add to his larder. He had not taken anything in some time and it gnawed at him. Gertie had been strictly instructed to keep heading north toward Potato Patch while he checked out the rider. Cain had figured he could use a couple more horses since his pinto was showing signs of wear and was not up to extended travel. Riding in the wagon with Gertie and the "snotty nosed whiners", as he called them, was not to his liking. He put the spurs to the horse again and slapped him with the rein ends. Although obviously tired and sweaty, the game animal tried harder.

The rider had disappeared into the copse, without spotting Cain. He kept pushing his horse. As he neared the grove, Sharpe slowed down and edged the cayuse into the trees. The animal was trembling from his exertions. Cain was thinking he soon would have another and better horse. He dismounted and lapped the reins over a bush. He moved forward cautiously toward the other two horses he could see ahead. The rider was not in sight but he heard limbs breaking over to his right. The unsuspecting man was gathering deadwood for a fire. Willy Sharpe sneaked closer, drew his gun, and when the man straightened up, shot him twice in the back. He pitched over on his face, jerked a few times and lay still. Willy came forward and turned him over. A man in his thirties with several days growth of beard. Nothing unusual. Willy went through his pockets and took out about seventy dollars in bills, two twenty dollar gold pieces and some silver. "Not too bad," he thought. He then stripped the body and scalped the drooping head. Pushing the deadwood into a pile and, after looking around carefully, he started a fire. When it was blazing he tossed in the blood stained coat and shirt, took a heavy stick and pushed the fire into tight conflagration and added the scalp. He settled back on his heels and watched until all signs of hair and clothing were gone. He scattered the embers and gathered up the remaining clothing and with a leafy branch swished the ground as he backed away eliminating footprints. When he got to the horses he went through the saddle bags and packs and was disappointed in finding no more money. A little food and can goods, and miner's tools was all. He folded the clothes, stuffed them into a saddle bag and after mounting the riding horse, brushed away his remaining footprints. It was a sorrel gelding and appeared stronger than his pinto. He took the branch and made certain he had eliminated his last marks and turned back toward his own animal. He reached over and got the reins of the pinto and tied them to the pack horse. He started back for the wagon, dropping the branch at the edge of the copse.

Gertie had lumbered on with the wagon for about an hour before stopping. Firewood came from the canvas sling under the wagon and she started cooking. The kids were fed and she was straightening up when Cain returned with his loot. He looked at the kids napping under the wagon and the embers under the pot and asked, "What's for supper?"

"Some mulligan stew," Gertie replied.

"Good, I'm hungry."

"Where'd ya get the horses?"

"Some poor bastard must have been waylaid by Indians."

"Yeh, who went off and left his horses." She was curious to see what story he would tell this time.

"Don't know; they could have been scared away."

"And not caught by Comanches? You'd better come up with a better story," she cautioned.

"Well, that's the one I'm stickin' with."

The kids were stirring. They had heard the exchange and both knew Benedict had done something awful again. Moving uneasily, they huddled closer to each other.

"You kids stay quiet and don't make no trouble," loud and gruffly from Benedict.

Sally turned over and pulled closer to Joey. Joey patted her on the head and made soft noises.

"We can sho use them extra horses. Glad I found 'em. Didn't see nothin' of the guy who had 'em. That old pinto of mine was going sour. He'll have a chance to straighten up now. This here stew ain't half bad, Gertie. You always could cook.

Gertie just snorted. Compliments were rare.

"Ought to be gettin' into Potato Patch tomorrow. Maybe we can squat there for a while. Just as well stay here for the night. I'm feelin' a might tired. Not as peppy as I used to be."

While unhitching the horse from the wagon, he continued, "Wish I had a mule. 'S better for a wagon than a beat ole hoss." The beat ole hoss was the worn down remains of the high stepping black with the three white stockings that Cain had taken from the Allen place. Lindsey Benedict was hard on his mounts, many of them dying under his neglect. He unsaddled the sorrel and pinto and took the pack down from the grulla. He made no effort to rub them down; just tethered them near the wagon, not even caring if there was enough forage. Gertie watched him with disgust and grunted.

"What's bothering ya, ole woman?"

"You are. You don't know how to take care of no horses. You just kill 'em."

"Well I don't see ya doin' no betta."

"Well I will." Gertie got up and settled the animals down some distance apart. She came back to the wagon, took down the bucket, filled it with water from the cask on the side of the wagon and took it to each of the animals in turn. They drank thirstily and she made another round.

"Don't give 'em all our water."

"Shut up. We got plenty."

"Don't shut me up you ole harridan. I'll lambaste ya one."

"Just try it. One of these times you'll go too far, Willy."

"You shut up, ole woman."

Gertrude went to the wagon and crawled in. She spread out the

115

pallets for the youngsters and said, "Come on now, it's time for bed. Bad to be sleeping down there on the ground after dark. Come on in here now." The youngsters climbed into the wagon and stretched out on the pads. Gertie spread a blanket over them. "Yawl go on to sleep, now. Good night."

"Come on Gertie. You and I can make out here under the wagon."

Gertie threw other blankets and a pillow to the ground and came down and spread them under the wagon, stripped off most of her clothes and stretched out. Cain, after putting his pistol belt on a wheel, discarded his coat, shirt and pants then snuggled down beside her.

CHAPTER 21

YOUNG GEORGE CAME GALLOPING BACK with Sparta. Unlike many mules, Sparta liked to run. The long eared critter had gotten used to George, having removed some of his skin with hardy bites before settling down with his new rider. Sparta bit Doc only occasionally and now joined George into the seldom category. He enjoyed his chance to stretch out when George took him for a ride. Doc was not racing him as much as he had. Sparta was completely different from Ay's mule. Joshua could hardly be rushed and would run only with the most definite and vigorous encouragement. After racing, Sparta just needed a litle rest and then a suggestion and off he went again.

Sparta did not like any other quadruped in front of him and was like his brother Rastus, Doc's other fast mule. Rastus was a little faster than Sparta and remained the only animal that managed to stay in front of him on any consistent basis. It was Joshua's sole desire not to be in front and much preferred bringing up the rear, deliberately holding back until he was definitely at the end of the line. But now Sparta was performing true to form. He was headed back towards Doc's full out.

Aymond was up on the Widow's Walk, the circular balcony atop Doc's round study on the third floor. It had the best view around of the countryside. Aymond was lounging on one of the benches under the high gazebo turning often enough to keep the entire panorama in view. He had seen the dust patch to the west and had watched it dissolve into the charging George. Ay reached down and took Doc's binoculars from its case and focused it on the oncoming lad. He recognized George Allen but found it hard to absorb the change in him.

He showed no signs of injuries and seemed to be substantially larger. He replaced the glasses and hurried down to greet him.

George was not expecting Aymond and when he spotted him turned Sparta toward him and brought the mule to a quick stop as he came hurdling from the saddle. He grabbed Aymond by both shoulders and then hugged him hard.

"It's so good to see you again, Aymond! I didn't think you'd ever get back. Now we can get him. When do we leave?"

"Whoa. Slow down. Hold your horses. It's good to see you too, George. You look great and you've even grown some."

"Weigh twenty more pounds. When do we leave?"

"Hey now, I'm barely here. Hold on. We've got to figure out some plan and where to go. I plumb lost his trail and haven't the slightest idea where he can be. We need to do some talking. A little time now isn't going to make much difference. Glad you're heavier. It looks good on you."

"I's learned how to shoot, too. Doc got me a Winchester and taught me some tricks. I's not too fast on the draw with a pistol but I kin hit four cans out of six on a fence. I's ready to git him. Kin we leave tomorrah?" It was obvious what George had most on his mind.

"You've got a one track mind. I told you, we've got to figure out where to go rather than running in circles. We'll need to talk to Doc and get reports from all over. Cain's bound to leave his trace but it's no good for us to go charging out without some kind of plan. It shouldn't take long but we have to take the time to do it right. I know you're anxious and I won't take longer than necessary. Relax for a little while and let's do some thinking. Doc's down to the clinic, so you come on in and we'll get Mandy to hustle us up some grub. Put Spar away and come on in."

— — —

Doc put down his pipe and looked admiringly at Ay and George. George was eager to hit the trail while Ay was showing his maturity by waiting to figure some definite procedure. Aymond had been saying that they needed to find out if there had been any reported Indian attacks in any particular area. Doc repeated his information,

"Several have occurred down around Boonetown, but a number were reported over in New Mexico and Arizona. The reports indicated there were positive indications the ones there were the work of the Apaches. The ones at Boonetown could be Comanches or possibly the killer. I think we should wait a few more days and see what comes in from elsewhere or if there's some more activity around Boonetown."

"That makes sense, Doc. In the meantime, George and I can be getting together the things we'll be needing. I have Jericho and I assume George will be riding Apache. I can't see your letting him have Rastus."

"You're correct there," Doc agreed.

"Joshua'll do fine to tote the grub and extras. Think we should haul extra ammo so George can keep practicing. Won't need much in the way of camping equipment in this weather. Just a tarpaulin, slicker and bedroll. We'll both have Winchester and Colts shooting the same ammo, 40-40's. I'm taking a two shot derringer of the same caliber as a back up. Still have about two hundred dollars from my old stash, so no problem financially.

"George," injected Doc. "I'm going to advance you a hundred bucks in case you get separated from Aymond. Hold on to it and bring it back if you can. If you spend it, I'll let you work it out later."

"Golly, that's great of you Doc. I'll sho watch it."

"I know you will, son."

"I think I'll allocate a year to it, Doc. If I haven't had any luck in that period of time, I'll just have to chuck it as a bad deal and get back to my regular living."

"Sounds alright to me."

"I'll never give up," George chimed in.

"Of course you won't," allowed Doc while thinking, "Poor kid after a couple of years on a barren trail he'll need some real help adjusting." "Just remember you can come operate out of here," he added aloud.

"Really appreciate it, Doc."

"Well, nothing more to be accomplished around here now, so why don't the two of you take off on Jericho and Sparta and try a little shooting on the run. Can't be too good along those lines.

"OK, Doc. Come on George."

Doc went back to the porch where Cliff had spent most of his time in a chair. His leg had festered and Doc had cleaned it out two or three times. The infection had gotten to the bone, but other than severe pain, Cliff was finally on the mend. There had been no gangrene but it was almost impossible to put weight on his leg. His ribs were only hurting when he bumped or jerked but the leg was the main problem. Cliff had worried but Doc had reassured him. "Just time, son, just time. Infection's gone but the flesh has to heal from the bone out. Takes time but you'll be able to ride and walk as good as ever."

"Seems like forever, Doc."

"Keep reading those books and doing your math with Janey and it won't be wasted time. In fact, you're better off for it. Now stop worrying."

"I wanted to ride with Ay and George."

"And now you still know you can't for a while. Get with those books and quit giving me a hard time!"

Cliff picked up an opened copy of A Tale of Two Cities from the chairside table and began reading.

CHAPTER 22

WILLY AND GERTIE CAME DOWN THE
gentle slope into Potato Patch. There were no signs of empty or abandoned houses. In fact, a number of tents were in evidence. Some with wood fronts.

"Now Gertie, it looks like there's nothin' here we can move into. Have to put summin together on our own. Guess we just as well stay with the wagon 'til we decide if we're goin' to move on or stay."

"Don't look like much to me. There's an open space over there by the creek. At least we can be near some water."

"That's fine. I'll put the tarp up until we decide."

They rode over to the site and Willy stretched a rope between two cottonwoods, hooked the tarpaulin to it and anchored the other side to the ground. It would provide shelter in case of rain and there still was the wagon with its canvas top. Willy washed up in the stream, shaved, changed his clothes and felt free to wander down to the saloon. He buckled on his big Colt and shashayed down the main street. A few heads turned to take in the newcomer and he was careful to tip his hat to the ladies to make a good impression. He pushed into the saloon and looked around. There were cowhands at the bar, what looked like a couple of prospectors huddled over a bottle, and the solitary gambler in his frock coat dealing himself solitaire.

"Howdy, friend," he entoned, "How about a few cards?"

"Thanks, but not right now. Maybe later." He sauntered on up to the bar. "Beer. I'll take a long cool one."

"Best we can do, fellow," said the bartender taking a bottle out of tub filled with dirty water.

"It'll have to do then," as he took it and offered a half-smile.

The bartender pulled the cork and wiped the mouth with a dingy cloth. "Ten cents."

"My gosh. They're a nickel back down the road."

"Have to come farther," replied the barkeep laconically.

Willy took the bottle and sidled over to an empty table and settled in. Carefully, he took in the situation and wondered what he could do in Potato Patch. He did not have any real training in anything, having lived by his wits since he was little. He wondered if the saloon could use some more help, but it did not look prosperous. No piano, no mirror. Just a long crude bar and rough tables with chairs well enough finished to look out of place. He sipped on his beer and continued his musings. The gambler came over and asked if he could sit down.

"Feel free," Willy responded.

"My name's Aaron Mirestes. Excuse my prying and tell me to mind my own business if you think I'm out of place but I wondered if you're wandering through or if you're going to stop."

"Don't know yet. My name's Willy Sharpe. Just got in with my wife and kids and looking for a place to light. What kind of town is this and what sort of work is available?"

"Growing, growing. What sort of work do you do?"

"Just about anything." Which meant just about nothing. Willy never wanted to work unless he had to.

"Livery man needs some help," Aaron offered. "Lot more traffic coming through these days and he's added on to his stables but doesn't have anyone to assist him. He was bitching about it yesterday."

"Might do for me. I appreciate your interest."

"Did it more for Joe. Joe Hughes. He's the livery. His place is down the street on the left and behind the stores. Go talk to him."

"Sho will," said Willy taking a pull on his bottle. He took two more big slugs and then finished it off. Wiping his mouth he added, "Thanks, friend. I'll remember it." He headed out the batwings and swung left.

Joe Hughes, a monster of a man, was sitting in front of his stable. The unpainted new wood of the addition shone through like it had been given a fresh coat of cream. Joe was tipped back in his chair, hat over his face, enjoying a noon siesta. Willy hated to bother him but Joe was a light sleeper and awoke when he heard the footsteps and pushed up his hat. "Howdy."

"Didn't mean to bother you, but Aaron Mirestes said you might be needing some help."

"Sure do. You looking for a job?"

"Need to. My name's Willy Sharpe. Got a wife and two kids camped over by the creek. What'll it pay?"

"Twenty dollars for the first month and thirty after that, if you work out. Know much about livery work?"

"A little. Know summin' about horses. Can keep 'em rubbed down and fed. Cleaned up some muck in my day."

"That'll sure do for a start. I'll show you some other things. Want to start tomorrow?"

"Sure, but I'll need to clear it with my ole lady first. She's been wantin' to stop for a while. I'll take a look around if that's all right."

"Sure, help yourself." Joe's big barn was well organized. There was a lockable tack room which doubled for sleeping, a large number of separate stalls, a hay room with a hay loft just above, a separate large room with three wagons and a couple of buggies. About half the stalls were full and the corral in the back penned about fifteen horses. Joe was ready for more trade. Obviously Potato Patch was thriving.

Lindsey thought, "This should do for a while. The work shouldn't be too hard and the worse part would be shoveling the horse shit. He could make Joey help with that." He smiled. "I'll see you in the morning, Mr. Hughes. About what time?"

"Six is fine. Usually about seven-thirty in the winter. And call me Joe."

"Sure, Joe. See you at six."

Willy returned to his wagon and told Gertie of the job offer. It suited her, but she was not too pleased with Willy's idea of having Joey help. "That boy needs some schoolin'."

"What good it do'im? He ain't gonna be no doctor or lawyer. Needs to larn to work wid his hands."

Gertie quieted down. She would handle that situation when it came up.

"Since we're stayin' for a while, we jest as well fix us a sod hut. Can't live unda this tarp forever. Let's go pick a spot." Willy hated the idea of the work required to build a sod hut but felt it would establish his image as a settler. That, and helping in the livery stable. He could tell traffic was on the increase and could provide him with amble opportunities to skin the tenderfeet.

Gertie said, "Ain't nothin' wrong with this spot. Got water, shade and plenty of mud with turf everywhere."

"Yeah. It'll do." Willy walked over and picked up some loose sticks, came back to the wagon and fumbled out a heavy hammer and some twine. He hammered a stick in the ground, looked around to get his bearings, and then stepped off about seven long paces and hammered in a stake shaped limb. He then marked off five paces at a right angle and knocked in another. After another right turn he went seven paces and looked to see if he was even with the first marker. Satisfied, he hammered in the last stick. Taking the twine from his pocket he tied a knot and stretched the string to the first stick. Tied it again and went on around. Gertie watched with keen interest. She had never seen a sod house built and wondered how it was done. She knew it had to be simple. Willy got the wheelbarrow from where it was fastened under the wagon and took out the wrapped tools inside it. Willy had always stolen and looted with discretion. He had packed away anything he thought would be useful and had left caches well hidden as he traveled along, figuring he could come back and retrieve them some day or they would be there if he needed them. He was a natural packrat. Gertie knew of a few of the caches but not most of them since Cain was essentially a lone and secretive person.

Dropping the tools in the back of the wagon and removing the shovel from the outside edge he then trundled to a patch of green grass. With the shovel he cut out blocks about a foot and a half long, a foot wide and eight inches deep. When he had tried to go a foot deep, the sod kept tearing. It lifted easier with the slighter depth. He loaded the barrow and headed back to the cabin site, stopped, and put a piece down in the front middle with its back touching the string and then moving a pace to his right, he set another.

"That's where the doorway is," he told Gertie. After he had set down enough sections to have reached the first stake, he yelled at the boy, "Joe, come here and watch how this is done. Gertie you watch too," he added.

Going back to his digging spot, he found it much easier to remove the turf when there was an open space adjacent. He sliced down from the top to cut the shape and then lifted it out from the other side with the shovel pushed under. All of this was under the interested eyes of the boy and Gertrude.

"Come on." He returned to the open space for the doorway and cut one section in half, placed it on top of the one by the doorway and then set the rest in a staggered line with the middle of the top row one being over the joint of the sections underneath making a strong bond. Mud was added from a bucket if the pieces were not damp enough. He finished setting out sod and emptied the debris remaining in the wheelbarrow on the ground. "That's how it's a done. Now Joey, let's see whaja kin do."

Joey took the shovel and pushed the wheelbarrow back to the hole, determined, but lacking experience in digging. He pushed down the shovel but his lines were not straight and the sod broke badly in trying to lift it. "You're not tryin', ya damn slacker," shouted Willy. "Gertie, show'im how." Gertie was just as inexperienced but she was wily and had an adult's strength. She managed to get one out whole even though not so smooth as Willy's.

"That's good," Willy conceded. "I'll do the rest." He had noticed some people standing on the road watching. The barrow filled quickly and he added another row along the front. "Whiles I'm at the stables y'all kin work on the back 'til ya get it down betta."

With his pipe out and lighted, he squatted in front to admire his handiwork. The front already looked like a wall. "Gertie we kin lift the sod from inside the walls to make a hard dirt floor and it'll help furnish sections for the back walls. We'll leave a section open on the side to put in a fireplace. We kin cook outside fa now. I'll haul in some rocks for a chimney and fireplace." Willy was thinking that they might be long gone by winter if he could make a real hit. He just needed to find one set of rich ones traveling through.

Things were looking up for Cain.

CHAPTER 23

GEORGE AND AYMOND CAME CHARGING across the sage, avoiding clumps and depending on their experienced mounts to stay clear of holes and snags while they watched for jack rabbits. Their ongoing game allowed George to take the first two shots, then Ay had two and then it was back to George and so on. George seldom got to take his second set. Aymond was unbelievably good on the run while George was showing definite improvement: hitting one in five, not bad for an apprentice. George could no longer be termed a novice.

A rabbit jumped up on the right ahead. George turned quickly in pursuit and brought out his pistol with a rapidity that bespoke diligent practice. There was a pause and then two bangs in quick succession. George had missed and Aymond quickly drew and, with one shot, skewered the animal. George was despondent. "I'll never get it down."

"You're taking too long, George. As I've told you before, draw, point and shoot. Quit taking time to aim. I've told you this time and time again. You hit some, aiming, but you'll never be consistent with a moving target like that. You'll also miss a lot with the fast work practice but it'll come to you after a while. Take my word for it. Just point and shoot. Let your reflexes take over. We'll keep trying. You notice I miss now and then but keep my average way up. Don't let it get you down. Just keep working." George was using up a lot of ammunition but Doc kept encouraging him and providing all the shells he needed. Aymond used his share but not as many as George. Shooting well continuously meant a lifetime of practice.

"Say, Ay?"

"Yeah."

"You said sompun' funny to Doc back there."

"Well?"

'It sounded like 'oh kay'. What do that mean?"

"Didn't realize I said it. It's OK. It means every thing's fine or all right. It come from the OK Club started by some fellows working to get Martin Van Buren elected President again. It was named after his birthplace Old Kinderhook and gradually got to meaning things were looking up or were all right. It was spreading around Charlottesville and the University."

"I see," mused George. "Well, I'm oh kay."

"Wouldn't think so," laughed Ay.

— — —

The sod house was progressing well. Willy had bought a few rough boards to frame the windows and doors, the part of it he was always careful to perform while the neighbors could watch. It was gaining him a reputation for being a hard worker and good provider while he kept up his deception of being a prospector by going off on weekends with pans, pick and other paraphernalia. He saw to it that the word was widely spread that he was looking for gold. Everybody understood this. It was part of their way of life. He shot game while on his treks and let it get around he was a good hunter, being careful to share portions of his kills with neighbors and townspeople.

When, after several months, a man came through from Boonetown with rumors of Cain's capers, they were quickly dispelled by Gertie, who would tell that when the kids were sick and needed fruit, Willy had stolen oranges for them when none of the hoarders would sell them any. That the fellow he took them from was so ashamed he came and brought the children some. This enhanced Willy's reputation as a good provider. A few retained a dubious attitude. Sometimes western rumors had real kernels of truth behind them.

Willy dragged in a huge pine log, and enlisting the help of several neighbors, lifted it to the pointed ends of his house and settled it in as a first class ridgepole. The saplings running from it to the front and back walls were interwoven with others parallel to the ridgepole and then thatched with long grass and reeds. On top of it all he put thin layers of sod. It stayed remarkably cool in the summer and he knew it would be toasty warm in winter.

Gertie and the kids settled in. It was the first home Sally knew or remembered. Joey had faint recollections of one but it was hard to focus on. There were two big beds. One in the back corner for the kids and larger one in the front corner for Willy and Gertie. Both had a rack hung with a cloth that shut off the beds. Meals were assigned to the other end, near the fireplace opening, where a rough-hewn table with four chairs of Willy's manufacture provided surfaces for most domestic purposes.

While Willy worked at the stable, Gertie taught the youngsters their spelling and arithmetic lessons. Somehow, she had managed to scrounge a few books, including fairy tales and a *Mother Goose*. For Joey there was *Ivanhoe, A Tale of Two Cities*, and *Paul Bunyon*. There was also a Bible. Gertie was happy with the situation. "Oh Willy, can't we just stay here. You've got a good job and with the way this place is growing you can get your own stable or buy Joe's. This'll be a good life for us, Willy."

Willy just snorted for he had no intentions of staying in this hole of a place since he longed to be someplace like San Francisco with real money in his poke and to enjoy some real living. Time would come when he could cut out from Gertie and those bastard kids and leave them here to rot if they liked it so well. But Willy was too canny to let Gertrude know what he was thinking. He even backed off some of his rough behavior. He still cussed the kids and threatened them but never really tried to attack them as he had in the past. Now and then he gave Joey a spanking when he failed to perform as ordered. This was over Gertie's objections, but he countered with, "Spare the rod and spoil the child," and Gertie had quieted down.

About mid-summer Cain had loaded his prospecting outfit, headed out and taken over a two-day journey to the west, farther than he had been before. As he approached some hills he noted a man coming out of the trees leading a burro. He was singing and grinning. "What's the joke, old-timer?" he inquired.

The grizzled prospector immediately hushed, straightened up and looked suspiciously at Cain. He had been fortunate in panning metal in a creek and finding a vein upstream. It had been a rich strike and the donkey probably carried almost twenty pounds with much more still available back at the dig. He had made no effort to stake his claim but had carefully covered all signs of digging and waited for a rain to finish the job of concealment. With old wisdom he knew this was by far the safest way to protect his interest. That same wisdom was now berating him for betraying his happiness to a stranger. Little did he know how dangerous this stranger was. His quick glance at the burro's pack had not been missed by Cain and Cain had drawn the right conclusions but knew he must conceal his thoughts. "You sound just like my ole man. Dad used to sing all the time he traveled. I never knew where he got all that air," lied Cain. The old man relaxed. That was a grand explanation and he bought it.

"Always did like to yodel on my way. But mine comes from me Irish mither. Wasn't a time she weren't singin'. Sure and begorra makes the miles ga easier." He thought the situation well handled and in control, but he had underestimated Cain.

"Well, ole fella, you do warm my heart. Yep you doou remind me of ole Dad. What a lad with a tune he was. Sure miss those harmonies. Let's stop a few minutes and let me fix you some hot coffee. On a hot day it goes down good after a morning's trudge. Let's just settle down while you warble some."

"This ought to soothe him," Cain thought. He gathered some wood and started a small fire. He got out the coffee pot and makings. The oldtimer had been lulled. He had been out of coffee for weeks and eagerly anticipated the treat.

"Haven't had no coffee in some time. Sho will be good."

"I've got a little extra. I'll let you have some."

"That's sho kindly of ya, ole scout. Mighty kindly," relaxing even more.

Cain watched the pot come to a boil, got up and took out a cup.

The oldster interposed, "I got mine, young fella. You hold on to ya own. Kind enuff for ya to furnish the brew."

"You first." Cain poured a cup full for him, watched him take a satisfying gulp and then settle back. Cain filled his cup, turned quickly and tossed the scalding liquid in the prospector's face.

"Wha', wha'," screamed the old man, the coffee running down his face and grizzled beard. His eyes had taken the full blast of the fiery fluid and felt like hot pokers taking away his sight. Cain pulled his lariat from his horse and tied the man's arms behind him while pulling him up to a small tree to which he fastened him. The man continued to scream and holler. Words were becoming recognizable. "Why'd ya do that ya bastard? Wha' the hell's wrong with ya? I ain't done nuddin to you. Wha's wrong with ya?"

Cain walked over to the burro and opened a canvas bag. Sure enough, stuffed full of glowing yellow which was mighty heavy. Satisfied, he turned back to his victim. He opened his canteen and put some water in his cup and splashed it into the man's face and then opened a tin of bacon grease and smeared it on. "Quieten down and let me fix you up." He just moaned. "Where ya get this stuff?" The old man continued to moan. "Tell me where ya got it or I'll really give ya something to yell about." Just groans and moans. "I said tell me where ya got it."

"Won't"

"We'll see about that." Cain went behind and lifted his arms with the rope. He screamed and passed out.

"Damnation, you idjut! Stay awake!" Cane looked around and noted some willows farther down. He untied the man and slung him across the jackass, then mounting his own animal, led it toward the willows. Sure enough, his luck was holding. There was a small stream. Cain lifted off the prospector and threw him into the branch. He thrashed around, sputtered, and came up for air. Cain pulled him ashore and shouted, "Now talk."

"Won't" The man began to realize he could see blurred shapes. The fact he was not blind gave him added determination not to give the bastard what he wanted, even if it meant death.

The frustration was showing on Cain as he pulled out his gun and threatened, "I'll shoot off your balls if you don't tell me."

"No ya won't."

"I'll show ya, ya stinking bastard."

"You're the bastard."

Cain, in his anger, fired without his usual deliberation and watched in horror as the lead went into the man's chest instead of his groin. He had shot too quickly. The old grubber grunted and keeled over. "Oh, shit, now I've killed 'im." In his furor he turned and shot the donkey. Then realized how stupid that was. Now his horse would have to carry the extra weight and slow him down. "I've got to get control of myself. This won't do. I'll leave myself wide open if I keeps doin' things without thinkin'. Slow down and get ahold of yaself!"

Cain sat for a few minutes then got up and gathered limbs from the deadwood with which he started a large fire and put the coffee pot on the side. He scalped the old man, shoved his body in the creek, tossed the scalp onto the fire and watched it burn. Next, he butchered the donkey. Indians liked mule meat and sometimes donkey almost as well. He buried the portions over a wide area and threw a haunch on the fire, watched it burn down to the bone, took his sleeping bag and went off several hundred yards into the woods. This was no time to be nosed out by Indians. With a briar patch for protection, he spread his sleeping bag, crawled in, and fell asleep. When he awoke he went back to the fire site and was pleased to see just remnants of the bone and ash. He scattered the ashes, mounted and moved out, still cussing himself for having to carry the extra weight but thinking maybe it would make the Indian attack look more real.

No one noticed anything when he dragged back into Patch. He just looked worn out from prospecting and was careful not to show any signs of exultation over his gold. In fact he was still fuming because he had not been able to drag the location of the lode from the prospector. "Damn no good. He shudda talked. Jist no sense. Well he got wat was acomin' ta 'im."

He unsaddled his horse and hung the saddlebags on a peg under the leanto where he kept hay and gear. He figured no one would bother them there and he could hide the gold later.

"That would sho take care of me in San Francisco. Now to add a little bit to it and I can take off. I'll havta keep it hid from Gertie. She'd want to go and she's gittin' to be too much of a problem especially with them kids. Gotta find some place I can stash this stuff so she won't find it. That'll hold 'til later. I'm hungry now."

Gertie had heard him coming and had ladled out some hot stew full of meat and fresh vegetables. He shoveled them down. "Goin' ta miss her cookin', he thought. "But there'll be better grub in Frisco."

CHAPTER 24

GENERALLY AYMOND SLEPT LIGHTLY BUT at home he relaxed and allowed himself the luxury of deep slumber. Doc shook him by the shoulder. "Ay, wake up," and as he stirred, "There's been another Indian attack down at Potato Patch. Some old prospector was killed and scalped. Ate his burro. Couple of odd things, boot marks in some spots and a shod horse. May have been made by somebody later but whoever it was didn't bury him."

"May have been scared for his own skin or it might be Cain. Worth taking a look. George has been getting me restless, Doc, and this'll give us something to do. Shouldn't take long to check it out. We can leave tomorrow morning."

"Get with it, Aymond," Doc teased with a laugh. "It'll get you out from under my feet. Never seen such moping around."

Aymond took off to tell George the news. He was standing near the corral practicing his draw and looked up when he saw Aymond approaching. "I'll never git as fast as you, Ay. I jist can't git it down right."

"Just keep working and don't give up. You're worlds faster than when I first got back. Besides, you've still got some growing to do with more coordination to settle in. Practice, like you're doing and you'll get there, and surprise, I've got some good news. There's a possible fake Indian attack down at Potato Patch and we're going to check it out. Leave first thing in the morning. Check out ole Sparta and Jericho and pack your saddle bags. Bring plenty of extra ammo. I'll hustle up a food pack from Mandy and check out Joshua too. He'll be needed. We don't know how long we'll be gone. Shouldn't be too long but you never know."

Ay headed for the house while George was climbing over the corral gate.

"Mandy, George and I are taking off after that Cain fellow again. May not be gone too long but you never know, so we're taking Joshua. We'll need grub for a couple of weeks and fixed up to fit the pack saddle. You can take care of us can't you?"

"You knows I can, Mister Ay. Make you some good fixin's for the first few days."

"Always could count on you, Mandy," with a sudden hug that pinned her arms.

"Get off with you, boy, whiles I got work ta do. No mo of ya playin' around."

She laughed and Aymond laughed back. Mandy had been after him since he was twelve and had warmed his bottom a number of times with Doc's full approval. They shared a gentle love. She and Mary Jane O'Kelly had been his surrogate mothers. Aymond had always attracted mothering, even Soft Wind of the fierce Comanches had yielded to his attractions. It had been the same with the Apaches. Green Willow had included him with her sons. She and Hawk Scream had treated him like a born Apache. All his tangled relationships still bound Aymond and he was proud of them. He sorrowed at times because he had never seen Soft Wind or Green Willow again. He could barely remember his own parents.

Mandy shooed him on out of the kitchen and into the front of the house where Doc was preparing to go to the clinic. "Got some diphtheria among the school kids. It's contagious so you stay away. Cheer up Cliff; he needs it. Janey should be along shortly and I'll ride over with her. Wish I could talk that woman into marrying me. She likes, nay, even loves me well enough, but is muley headed on the issue. As you know, she says marriage is fatal to her husbands. I certainly don't agree. Just because she lost three so quickly is no sign I'm going to keel over after the knot's tied. Try talking some sense into that woman's head. She needs to know it's all rot. It's tough being lonely like this and her being so close all the time. Apply those Indian intuitions and college stuffed head of yours to the problem and get it solved for me. I've been working on it for at least eight years and a reef stuck schooner can make more progress than me."

Happy noises from the kitchen made them realize the subject of the conversation, Mary O'Kelly, had arrived. They both hurried down the hall while Mary turned and grabbed Aymond as he came in. "Heard you're going, Ay. Maybe you'll have better luck this time, but I can't say the addition of George and Cliff to the household was bad luck."

"Be better luck if you'd go on and marry Doc. It gets bad listening to him bemoan his fate," said Aymond directly. "You need to quit stringing that man along, Molly."

"He strings himself along. I've told him firmly for years that I can never marry him. I like him better as a live friend." The multi-widow, now past her middle thirties, was most bequiling. She even had Aymond, who did not think of her romantically, entranced with her looks and vivacity.

"Ah, Molly, the time has come for you to give up your dumb notion. The war and circumstances did you in on those others. It's just superstition. Nothing's going to happen to Doc if he corrals you except to make him a happy man."

"Did Doc, put you up to this?" she asked, knowing full well he had.

"Can't deny it but I believe it on my own. You're a perfect pair and Doc needs you. The years are slipping away for him and he's realizing it. You're torturing the man. You're always so near around and yet really so remote. Do right, woman, and marry that harassed soul!"

"You're mighty persuasive young Ay, but I have to hold out."

"You'll never get it through that thick but very pretty skull that I've been demonstrating that he's more likely to expire if you don't marry him. Anyway, as Mandy told you, I'm off after Cain again. When I get back I want to see the two of you cohabiting as is correctly proper at your age. Loosen up Molly and grab him."

Molly laughed, "Get on with you, boy. Doc, oh Doc, come get this John Aldrige off my back."

Doc came in and Molly allowed, "Almost persuaded!" and with a giggle, "Suppose I said, 'Speak for yourself, Ay.' Would serve you right. Now send him on his way and you, you underhanded little manipulator, come ahead and let's move on to the clinic." And louder, "Mandy we're gone. Come on, Doc," grabbing his hand. She winked at Ay as she went out the door.

Aymond headed to the porch to tell Cliff. He knew how badly the youngster wanted to be up and going but his leg had just started to mend and there was no way. He would just have to chirp him up and get him contented with "next time." A hard job.

CHAPTER 25

WILLY HAD SLIPPED BACK TO THE SOD HUT when he had seen Gertie taking the kids to the store. He hastily dug a hole where the hearth was to go. The opening in the wall had been closed with a piece of heavy canvas while Gertie continued to cook outdoors. Her stove was a sod "U" with a grill across the top and was located just outside the front door. Gertie had not been comfortable with the arrangement where the neighbors could watch her doing the kitchen work but Willy was not moved by her pleas. He had worked enough and saw no sense in preparing for winter when he had full intentions of being long gone before then. He told Gertie he would fix it before it got cold but she continued to grumble. He had decided that the situation could provide him a hiding place.

He finished with the hole and went to the leanto for the gold. He returned and dumped it down, covered it over, and then smoothed the surface. He would pile some stones on it that evening and tell Gertie he was starting the fireplace. He returned to the livery stable much pleased with himself.

But he had neglected to take in Gertrude's acuity and keen sight. When she came in, she smelled the scent of fresh dirt which puzzled her. She stepped out the door and inhaled. Nothing out there. She came back in and caught it again instantly. There was definitely the smell of fresh earth. She slowly circled the room breathing carefully. She went outside and around to the canvas covered spot and inhaled. Nothing.

"It must be inside, and in the chimney place," she thought. "Why am I wasting time on this?" But her curiosity was strong. She glanced around and saw the children playing some distance away.

She went back inside and over to the chimney opening. Nothing unusual. She continued to look and noticed some dirt pellets over near the outer edge. She got up and picked out a large kitchen knife and started sticking the ground. On the right hand side near the front it went in easily.

"Ah hah, that bastard has been up to something while I was gone." She dug down and found the deerskin bag. Pulling it up she was surprised by the weight but had figured it out by the time she had it open. "My God, must be enough to buy five steamboats, or maybe two Texas ranches with full herds." She tied it back and carefully reburied it being certain the ground was smooth.

She was not surprised when Willy came in and glanced at the opening, but he did not notice her watching. And she also was not surprised when he suggested starting the fireplace. He took the buckboard and commanding Joey to come along collected enough smooth surface rocks for the hearth. He took the stones to the outside of the opening and picked up a heavy knife and hatchet from the leanto. He proceeded to dig out the earth and set the stones in place. He started a few on their sides to start the fireplace and quit when the stones ran out.

"That'll do for now. I'm tired and I'll do the rest lata. Joey mix up some mud and put it in da cracks. Some of that clay by da sycamore o'er there by da crick edge should do. Get Sally ta help. She'll like playin' in da mud."

The children filled in the spaces between the stones with the wet clay and Willy told Gertrude that a small fire would harden it. Gertie built the fire and thought how shrewd Willy was. The hearth would show no signs of moved stones or disturbance. The gold was effectively hidden.

Satisfied with his day's accomplishments, Willy decided he owed it to himself to get mildly drunk. He had been careful with his drinking after getting in serious trouble and Gertie usually kept him from major disasters. He went down to McKenzie's bar and ordered a bottle. MacKenzie was surprised since Willy now had a reputation for hard work and sobriety. Tonight he proceeded to tie one on. When the bottle was about two-thirds gone he began to get noisy and wandered over to the poker table. The everplaying crowd was there and had been at it since about four that afternoon. They were not happy with the gratuitous loud advice Willy started giving. Then it hit them. Here was some fresh meat acting without caution.

"Have a seat and join in," invited Martin, the largest of the players as he scooted his chair over. "Bring a chair from the next table." Willy was happy to do it. He had been treading the straight and narrow in Patch so long he felt he deserved diversion. He sat down and began making all the wrong plays. He drew to inside straights, stayed in large pots with small pairs and bluffed too often. He lost two months wages in a matter of half an hour while simultaneously finishing off the bottle becoming louder and louder and then belligerent. The crowd went along with him while he continued to play stupidly and lose rapidly. When he had no more funds they told him to get lost. Maddened, he stood and drew his Colt and shot a hole in the ceiling while yelling that they'd been cheating him. MacKenzie pulled out his double barrel while Martin clobbered Willy's wrist and scooped up his gun when it hit the floor. "No problem," Martin insisted, while clobbering Willy with the heavy Colt barrel.

Gertie had heard the gunshot and fearing rightly that Willy had drunk too much started running for the saloon. When she got in Willy was on the floor. The tap on the skull Martin had found necessary was effective in stretching Willy out cold.

"Oh no!" Gertie yelled.

"He's all right, ma'm," Martin assured her. "Just too much alcohol. He'll come around," purposely neglecting to mention his own part in the process.

Gertie knelt down beside Willy and began to stroke him. Realizing the possible problems, she added, "He can't help it. Whisky does it to him every time. He's a good, quiet man 'til that stuff gits 'im. Then he ain't good for nuttin' 'cept shootin'. Shouldn't be allowed to have it. I sho believe in them temperance folks. Whisky is the drink of the devil." She forced a tear down her cheek.

"Now, now ma'm. It ain't that bad. Just get him home and to bed. He'll be over it in the morning. Maybe a bad headache. We'll tell Mac not to serve him any more whisky. Hold him to beer and wine. Just take him on now."

Willy sat up and rubbed the side of his head. "What happened?"

"Had to much to drink, friend."

"It sho makes my head hurt," closing his eyes to the dim light.

"Think you can get him home ma'm?"

"Thanks, I'm sure of it. Jest help me git 'im up."

Martin grabbed him and jerked him to his feet. "Here he is all ready for the convoy home."

"Thanks again." Gertie slipped his arm around her shoulder and steered him out the door. She was satisfied with her performance. "I'm got 'em thinking he's only a wayward homebody."

Martin was satisfied too. "We taught that drunk ignoramus something. Don't come around fooling with real men. Those apron string types ought to stay home with their mothers. Well, we cleaned his plow. He'll never know where the money went."

Willy awoke the next morning with a splitting, swirling pain. He put his hand to his head and was startled by the large bump. "Where'd that come from?" Willy could remember little after getting the bottle. He settled back in the bed with a long moan.

Joe Hughes had heard about the escapade and felt Willy would not make it to work but waited until mid-morning to stroll over and check on him. Gertie met him at the door. "He's still suffering bad."

"Don't mean to pry but I heard the stories and just wanted to be sure he was surviving. He's a good worker so I don't mind an occasional toot."

"Thank you Mr. Hughes. He'll just have to sleep it off."

"Call me Joe. No need for formalities between us."

"Well, if you'll call me Gertie?"

"That's fine, Gertie. I'll leave you now. Tell Willy I dropped by and I'm not mad. Just tell him not to let it happen often."

Late that afternoon after he had managed to haul himself from the sack, he worked out what occurred. He had been set up. While drunk he had been pinochled. Clean lost the more than fifty dollars he had on him. He would get back on them some way. He just had to figure it out.

CHAPTER 26

GEORGE AND AYMOND MOVED OUT BEFORE daybreak. They started south while the sky was black with starlight and moved in a leisurely pace waiting for the glolight to show the wagon road south to Potato Patch. With the first touch of dawn Ay allowed Jericho to lengthen his stride and pick up the pace. George, on Sparta, kept easy company but Joshua was showing signs it was too early for a self respecting mule to be traveling at anything but a slow walk. Neither tugs on the lead rope nor loud, well directed exhortations did any good.

Deciding the issue needed to be handled early on during their travels, Ay passed the guide rope to George, and turning Jericho, moved back to encourage Joshua. As per his usual habits Joshua did not want another animal behind him and tried to turn to get behind Jericho but the tough grasp of George on the rope pulled him back. George took a couple of turns around the pommel to be prepared for what might come. Joshua tried to solve the difficulty by coming to a complete halt, but Sparta with encouragement from George kept on. Joshua's head was pulled forward and he strained back. Sparta strained ahead. Sparta was by far the better mule and Joshua was skidded forward. At that moment Ay added his bit by vigorously placing the end of his lariat to Joshua's end. The snapping line had an instant result. Joshua jumped forward and Sparta picked up speed. With his neck hurting and his buttocks stinging Joshua decided it was best to pick up the pace. Ay returned to the front reached and received Joshua's reins from George and settled down to an easy canter. Joshua decided he could revert to his old ways and put on the brakes.

"Needs another dose, George. Here, secure his lead." Aymond turned back while Joshua rolled his eyes as Ay went by. Fast pulling and sharp snaps with the lariat had Joshua back at a brisk pace in no time. He slowed once more about ten minutes later and Ay had only to hand the lead rope to George for Joshua to have another change of heart. He moved easily and as rapidly as the others after that.

Things were thus looking up when the edge of the sun showed easy on the left horizon. "We've really covered ground now that we've got that onery critter behaving," Ay laughed. He was enjoying the glorious morning. They kept moving fast and easy.

The two had covered about fifty miles when Ay spotted a large copse ahead and to the left. "Let's check," he said pointing. George assented and the small caravan changed directions. The group of trees surrounded a small spring and with water and some wood available they decided to bed down for the evening. They unsaddled their mounts and tethered them at nearby clumps of grass. George started gathering deadwood for the fire while Aymond took the pack off Joshua and began preparations for the evening meal. They had feasted earlier on ham sandwiches and a complete apple pie which Mandy had included. There still remained two more pies along with other delicacies. With the fire started Ay pan fried two steaks which had been carefully wrapped to prevent dripping. "This'll be our only fresh meat for a while unless we can shoot something. Haven't even been spotting jack rabbits." He sliced some potatoes with the skins on and added them to the skillet. He settled the coffee pot to the side of the fire and raked embers around it.

The food went down well and they decided to share a peach pie. With well-filled stomachs they scattered the ashes and spilled dirt on them. They separated and drew back into the woods about a hundred yards from the firesite and from each other. No use inviting disaster with obvious signs. Ay took Jericho with him to act as a watch dog. Jericho always reacted to strange noises and movements. There had been no signs of Indians or Comancheros, but caution costs little. George was learning.

The next morning they restarted the fire and fried bacon and cooked the half-dozen eggs Mandy had included. They heated her biscuits, which were beginning to get hard, in the bacon drippings. This combination had amused Ay's friends and made a few converts while in Charlottesville.

Deciding they would save the last pie until later in the day and cleaning up their campsite, they saddled the three animals and moved on. This time, Joshua conformed to the increase in speed with no filibuster.

They had gone about twenty miles when Ay drew up. He looked carefully at the ground and dismounted. He squatted and pulled at the grass and spoke in a firm voice, "Been a small group of Indians through here about three or four days ago. Unshod marks. Look here, George. You can make out the hoof marks but no sign of a shoe. The droppings are hard on the outside. George jumped down and examined the marks and dung. Three Trees was trying to teach him Indian tracking. George was an apt student and grasped much of what he was told and shown. That was why Three Trees, as he thought of himself when trailing, was pleased to show him the tricks. George was coming along and by the time he turned nineteen he should be right sharp. He would be a true man of the frontier: big, strong, fast, good shot and able to track. A grand combination. Although Three Trees was not as big as George would be, he would remain stronger, faster, a better shot and an incomparable tracker. He continued to hone his skills.

"We'll have to watch our back trail even more carefully and be doubly cautious when we crest a hill. Let's move on quickly. Although they rarely come back the same way they go, they could be in the area and we don't need any confrontations with Comanches now."

They moved south rapidly and had over sixty miles behind them when they pulled up at twilight. After the Indian signs, they had agreed on a fireless stop and munched jerky and pulled from their canteens. Ay took one of the big canteens carried by Joshua, poured the contents into his hat and watered the three animals. The mules were able to consume more. "Makes sense," he thought. "They're bigger."

The two were ready to settle down when Aymond remembered

the last pie. It was soggy but still sweet and appealing. "Glad you remembered it. I was ready for sack time," George allowed. They separated and stretched out to await the dawn.

Early afternoon found them approaching Potato Patch. Ay pulled up. I won't recognize him but you will. If you spot him stay away from him and don't let him see you. Don't do anything to call attention to yourself but just indicate him to me.

"We'll need to scout out the situation before we can do anything," Ay continued. "You know how he fooled the Matlocks and others and he could have done the same thing here. We don't want to stir up any trouble with the locals. Dad knows Brent Stephenson real well and he knows me. Some of the others might remember me but I'm not sure what side they would take.

"Cain won't know me or that I've been after him. At least I don't think so. He sure won't recognize me. He might recognize you but you've changed so much since his attack that I would doubt it. Whatever happens we've got to be sure he doesn't run until we can get him. I know you want revenge in the worst sort of way for your mother's sake, but let's get him hanged rather than being judge, jury and executioners," Ay cautioned.

"I'm going to take him, Ay."

"No you're not. You've got too much future to throw it away on a snake like this. Besides think about how it's going to affect him as he waits and waits to be dangling from a rope. That's real revenge."

"I'll slow kill him. That'll give him time to think."

"And will put you down on his level. Please, George, we've helped you, trained you, fed you, and have taken you in as one of us. Don't throw the fruits of our labors away. This will tear us up. Do you want to do this to Doc, Mandy and me? Think about it. We're your friends, George."

"Don't intend to hurt you. But I see that bastard in my nightmares. I've been livin' for this. Gotta do it."

"No you don't. Use some sense. Making him hang is just as good as shooting him. Makes him suffer longer and reaches the same goal."

"Oh Ay, my gut hurts so. I've gotta do sommum ta 'im."

"You're coming around. We'll take him together and ride him to Boonetown for the sheriff. We'll stay until they stretch him and you can even taunt him. He's got that coming."

"Just can't do it, Ay. I got to git 'im.

"Then you'll have to fight us first. Doc would be too upset with that. You're going to have to kill me before you do him in."

"Oh, Ay, I can't do that."

"Do me a favor. Let's do this the right way.

"All right, Ay. It's goin' to hurt but I'll try for now. If it don't work out, ain't promisin' I won't do summan else.

"Good man. Now this doesn't mean that if he takes after us we don't fight back. We just take him in a fair fight. My future depends on it and I hope that means something to you."

"It does, Ay."

"Good. Now, let's ride on in."

"If I see him I'll say, 'You need to get a mule, Ay.'"

"Sounds fine."

They soon pulled up in front of the saloon, dropped down and tied two of their mounts to the rail. Joshua was tied to Jericho. Recognition was instantaneous between Ay and MacKenzie. "Don't want no trouble," Mac rumbled.

"Won't get any, if you behave. Just passing through. I'd like to see Brent and Joe before I leave. Two fine men."

"Carpenter's out of town 'til tonight but Joe should be at the stables. Anything to drink?"

"Beer for me and milk for my friend." Doc had laid down the law for George. No alcohol until he was sixteen. Doc allowed the children at his table to have a small glass of wine at Christmas, Thanksgiving and Easter but otherwise nothing. He did not even serve them coffee until they were fourteen. George was used to it and thought nothing about it but it shook up the bartender.

"I ain't got no milk." He almost grinned, then he remembered other things about Aymond.

"Then get some from next door." Aymond looked evenly at MacKenzie. MacKenzie scurried out and returned after a short interval with a tall tumbler of milk. "Fine, and now I'll have mine."

MacKenzie poured a healthy slug into a big glass and left the bottle. "How much?"

"Six bits."

Aymond looked up slowly. He knew he was being over-charged. "Uh, thirty five cents. Sorry. I was thinking of something else."

"I bet you were." He counted out coins onto the bar, then turned and faced the poker players he had noticed coming in and recognized them as being the same ones from before. He laughingly thought, "Could have been here the whole time since I left." He bore them no animosity because they had been neutral in his fight. In fact, somewhat helpful. Finishing his drink, he said to George, "Let's go. I want to see Joe. He's the one who let me have the wagon and Liz to haul Cliff to Lizard Sands." They went out, mounted, and headed for the livery. They stopped outside the double doors and Ay dismounted and went in. A strange man was forking hay into one of the stalls. "I'm looking for Joe Hughes."

"Ain't around."

"Do you know where he is?"

"Nope."

"He still live here?"

"Yep."

"Don't talk much do you?"

"Sometimes. Ain't nuddin' to say now."

"Well, do you know when he might be back?"

"He kinda allowed it might be around sundown. He cudda gone with da carpenda. He's 'posed ta be comin' back at sundown ta."

George arrived at that moment, looked at the man and turned his back to him while facing Aymond, "You need to get a mule, Ay."

He exited rapidly with Aymond just behind him saying, "That shaggy thing of yours can't compare in any way with Jericho and you know it. You've got the high hat just because the Indians think that mule's tastier."

Returning to Cain he asked, "Can you put our animals up?"

"Sho can."

"We've got three. How much with a rub down and some oats or grain?"

"Six bits."

Pulling out a cartwheel, "Here's a dollar. Give them the extra special."

"Thanks, man. Will do," watching them leave. "Think they can buy anybody. Well, I'm outta here before long."

George and Ay walked to the edge of town. "So we've found him, George. I'm proud of you. Cool as a cucumber and gave me the precise info right on cue. Really proud of you. And didn't blink an eyelid. Now we'll make some discreet inquiries and find out what the score is."

"It was all I could do not to shoot 'im in the gut right then, that mother killin' bastard."

"I know friend but you handled it square. That's a real sign you've grown up. I really am proud of you and Doc will be too. But we've got to be careful and not let him get away this time. And that means shooting if he tries his violence again. We stay prepared. Let's get a bite now. There's a cafe next to the saloon that has pretty good food. Not Parisian, of course. Though, now and then, you do run into a French chef in these remote spots. This place has good basic fare."

They strolled back to the restaurant under the watch of the other walkers and standers. Aymond had been recognized and his feats were being expanded upon by the supposed knowledgeable. George and Ay went into the cafe and ordered from a grumpy, fat, middle-aged bedame. The late lunch, or early dinner, was grilled steaks with hash browns and skillet fried onions followed by several slices of fresh apple pie. Ay paid the bill and added a quarter for a tip. It got a smile out of the harridan. "How about some coffee, young lady?" Her smile got broader. "And some for my young friend, too." George grinned this time. The woman returned with two steaming mugs. Aymond put out another quarter and told her to keep the change although he was well aware that coffee was a nickel apiece with refills. The Amazon was turning into a Mother Hubbard. She solicitously wiped the table and asked how they had enjoyed the meal.

"Glorious," Ay proclaimed. "You must have baked that marvelous pie yourself."

Bullseye. She prided herself on her pies. She became even more amicable, patting him on the shoulder and saying "That's really kind of you to notice."

"It was our pleasure."

"Sho was," chimed in George, astonished at how Ay had changed the surly waitress into a hovering angel.

"You must find it rather confining to stay in here when there are such nice days outside," Ay continued the jaunty discourse.

"I takes it, but you're right I would rather be outdoors."

"Now a job like that fellow down at the livery stable would be better. Outdoors most of the time and able to stay in a warm barn in winter."

"Ain't so warm. And I wouldn't want to do the shoveling of stuff likes they got in a stable."

"You're certainly right. The fellow there seemed to be enjoying himself though."

"Oh, that's Willy. He's a good man. Two nice kids, but I can't say I'm much fond of his woman. Too stand-offish. No, I wouldn't want Willy's job."

"Not really right for a lady either, though I've seen other attractive young ones that seemed to take to it. Liked being around horses."

"Being around horses is fine if you don't havta clean up afta 'em."

"But more important, wouldn't want to lose your touch around here. Such grand pies!"

"That's right good of you."

"Well, we have to be rambling. Thanks again." As he stood, Ay left another quarter on the table. George grinned again and marveled at how Ay had made a lasting friend with some sweet talk and less than six bits. It was a lesson he would remember.

Once outside, Ay said, "We'll have to wait for Brent or Joe to get back to find out the details but he probably won't skedaddle before we're ready to move. Let's settle in the saloon and stay out of sight."

The poker players were still at it. Ay wondered at their staying power and how they managed to avoid all signs of labor. Mac called from the bar to see what they wanted. "Give me a cold one, if that's possible, and another milk for my friend." Mac muttered but headed

148

out to the cafe and was back shortly with the milk and a bottle dripping water. He put the milk in front of George and pulled open the top and set the bottle by Aymond. "Anything else?"

"How much?"

"Fifteen cents."

Aymond put down a half dollar and said, "Keep the change."

MacKenzie looked startled and grinned slightly. He could not figure that Aymond Bearman fellow. Then to himself, "And to think I tried to kill him. How dumb can you get?" He went back to bar.

When they had finished, Aymond got up and headed out. "Come on, George," who was already up and following. Outside Ay said, "Let's get our mounts and ride out a ways. We might learn something useful and it'll be better than stagnating in that bar."

"I'm game. I think I can even stand the sight of that man without givin' in."

"Shouldn't be getting around him anyway." They headed for the livery.

"Wait here, George. Won't do to take any chances. Stay out of sight and I'll get the mounts."

Jericho, Sparta and Joshua had been curried and fed and were standing with heads nodding in their stalls. Cain led Jericho and Sparta out of their cubicles, helped Aymond saddle them, opened one of the big double doors, and watched as Ay led them out.

"We should be back in an hour or two."

Willy watched him as he mounted and led the mule down the street where the youngster came out and also mounted. He wondered vaguely who they were and not having talked to any of the townspeople he was not aware of the stories being told about Aymond. Willy wouldn't have been interested anyway, having already checked the saddlebags and Joshua's load and knowing there was nothing worth taking except some bullets, which he resisted pilfering while muttering, "Mussn't be caught takin' things here." They also looked like they could take care of themselves. He had written them off completely as prospects. He cogitated on the younger one. Something was vaguely familiar. Shaking his head, he leaned his chair back and joined Joshua in sleep.

CHAPTER 27

AY AND GEORGE HEADED BACK AS THE SUN got low. Joe Hughes had preceded them and was sitting in front of the barn when they came up. "Howdy there, Joe. Glad to see you back."

"Why Aymond Bearman, did you just git into town?"

"Nope, been here since just after noon. Been riding around to kill some time until you got back. They told me you had taken off, probably with Brent, and shouldn't be back until nightfall."

"Brent and I got back early. We were checking a mining site."

"Need to talk to you on a bad matter. Is your assistant still around?"

"No. I sent him home just after I got back. He hadn't had a lunch break and had held the fort for me all day by himself. Good man, funny in some ways, but he's done his job around here."

"Took care of us too, but that's not the problem. He's a murderer, Joe."

"Couldn't be. Ain't caused a smidgen of problems around here, except for getting on a toot one night, but most of us have done that, though."

"Ain't that simple, Joe. He killed the mother and father of those two kids and burnt the wagon and left a trail of other killings behind him. What George here, had to watch while he did things to his mother, can't stand the telling. He almost killed George and left him for dead. He tries to make 'em look like Indian killings."

"Been only one Indian killing around here lately, and it was almost certainly an Apache killin'. Ate the donkey. Found a leg bone in the ashes."

"What about the other bones?"

"Never found them. Probably toted them off with the meat." Wait a minute, There was boot marks in the area. Thought it was someone coming through later but he didn't bury him. Scalped, too. Most likely Indians."

"More likely his work. We know what he did to George's mother and the lady at Haley's Crossing." It's all I could do to keep George from gut shooting him before you got back."

"I may do it yet. It took all the self control I had and Ay's sermon to keep me from it."

"What do you have in mind?"

"Didn't want to go off half-cocked. Want to be sure that the kids are not hurt. We don't know about the woman. Probably helping him. We want to take him to Boonetown for a trial. Most of the killings we know of were in Texas and they've got a sheriff and a judge. Won't take a jury long to find him guilty. There are other witnesses now that know the score. Take the woman, too, if she's involved. She doesn't seem to have been around during the killings we know of. He apparently picked her up along the way to look like a mother to the kids. Don't know why those youngsters haven't spilled the beans."

"They've told stories of him killing their father but Willy says they lived through the Indian attack and they think his rescue of them was part of it. They say there wasn't no Indians. Willy says they blame it on him for not being there to help fight off the Injuns but he says he knows for sure he was just lucky. Done no good. He'd just have been killed too. Too many of them Injuns. Nobody pays any attention to kids whose folks are killed in front of them. And besides, Gertie and Willy have been hard working. He's done a fine job around here. Hard to realize he's what you say."

"If it's affecting you that way, think what it does with someone who's never met us. I've been tied to a bed, threatened, almost spit on. But he's got to be stopped. He'd been caught long ago but he's sly enough to keep up his front, so we'd like you to help us but we can do it by ourselves if it makes you uncomfortable,."

"Let's talk to Brent. This is too much to take. It's too sudden.

Takes some getting used to. Come on, we'll corral Brent."

They walked to the carpenter shop with its signs, "Wood Work of All Kinds," "Coffins Made," "Burials Handled," and "Houses Built." Brent Stephenson was sawing away under a dull lantern. He looked up with surprise at Aymond, took in Joe, and wondered about George. "What brings you here?" he directed to Aymond.

"Bad news, Brent." Ay replied.

"Don't tell me Cliff died. I heard he was doing fine. In fact, I had a letter from Doc telling me what a good job I'd done."

"It's not that. Cliff's fine. It's the fact that Willy Sharpe is a cold blooded murderer, even though he looks harmless enough. He even killed the mother and father of those two kids. Oh yeah, Brent Stephenson, George Allen." They nodded. "George was anchored to a wagon wheel, almost dead when I came along on Willy's trail. George had been tied and made to watch what the bastard did to George's mother before he finally killed her. A real sadistic bastard! We called him Cain. Don't know what his real name is but I don't think it's Sharpe. We intend to take him into Boonetown for trial since they have a sheriff and a judge."

"Whoa, man, whoa. You're coming on too fast. You mean little Willy Sharpe is a killer? Hard to believe."

"That's why he was able to do what he did. Nobody thought he was dangerous until it was too late. But there's absolutely no doubt. It took all I could do to keep George from gut shooting him. We're taking him into Boonetown for a trial."

"Well it sounds reasonable enough. I'll help. I know who you are and what you can do. Probably won't need me but as quiet as Willy's been the town will need some convincing. We need to keep a low profile tonight. Don't want to cause any trouble around the woman and kids. We'll pick him up at Joe's in the morning when he comes in. Where you goin' to stay?"

"Hadn't thought. I'll pay MacKenzie to use his back room. One of these days you fellows will have a hotel. That's for you, Joe. Add a few rooms for sleeping to that barn of yours."

"I've got some sleepin' space in the barn. You and George better stay there. Willy gets in around six. Better if ya was there. Brent you need to come by at five-thirty. He won't be there 'til afta that."

"I've still got that chest to finish. So I'll take off and see you in the morning."

"Come on you two and I'll sho' ya your spot."

CHAPTER 28

JOE, AY, AND GEORGE WERE UP AND EATING eggs, bacon and biscuits when Brent came in. "Come join us," invited Joe.

"Nope. Had my breakfast already, but I will con you out of some coffee."

"Grab a mug and sit. We're having a council of war. Need to get ready. Willy could stroll in any time. We've about decided we'll let Aymond and George handle it and we'll stand by as backups. How's that strike you?"

"Seems reasonable. He might prove dangerous. He always packs that gun. Think we should have ours out?"

"Wouldn't think so. Might make him try something. Just let Ay and George grab 'im. They can be working on their horses—sorry George, forgot you were riding a mule. Anyway y'all can come up behind him and just grab 'im. He won't think nuddin of Brent and me sittin' here drinkin' coffee. I've got some rawhide here we can tie him with. After he's secure we can go see Gertie. My feelin' is we should take her too. She most have known about this stuff."

George piped up, "She wasn't helpin' against my ma. It was jist 'im. I don't take to hangin' women either."

"Why don't we wait and see what works out?" Aymond suggested.

"Fine with me," Joe agreed.

"Me too," from Brent.

"All right then," Joe said. "Brent and I will put our chairs over by the door and when we see Willy comin', we'll let ya know. That'll give ya plenty of time to be working on your horses, er mounts."

"We understand," said George with a chuckle.

— — —

Willy woke with a strange uneasiness. He turned over and growled, "Gertie git me some grub." Gertie was going to growl back but she thought of the gold and smiled to herself. Worth getting him some breakfast. She got up, pulled on her long gray dress, went outside and stirred the embers. Still some glow there. She added dry bark and kindling and put on the skillet. As it heated she went down to the stream where they had dug a small trench to divert some of the flow and inserted a rude slatted box. It served as a make-shift cooling box for food storage in pots and bottles. The kids were even calling it the spring house and played around it. She lifted the top and reached down and took eggs and a side of bacon from the large pail. She picked up the milk jug and replaced the box cover. Returning to the fire she sliced the bacon on a stump top which doubled as a work counter and dining table. They usually ate standing up. She had been onto Willy to provide a proper table and chairs but he kept putting it off, saying the ones inside were enough.

The odor of cooking bacon brought the children to the door. They went skipping down to the creek where they wiped off their faces and hands with a torn rag from one of Gertie's old dresses. This was a ritual Gertie insisted on and they had digested it into an old habit.

Willy came out still grumpy and uneasy. He could not figure it. He had his gold stashed in a fine hideyhole and nothing unusual had happened. He thought of the two strangers but they meant nothing. Maybe he had suffered a bad dream he could not remember. He finished his breakfast before the kids had barely started, drained his coffee cup and went inside and buckled on his gun belt. On a hunch he picked up his two shot derringer and fastened it to the loops in his sleeve. It had proved useful in the past for quick action against an unsuspecting opponent. Without saying anything to Gertie, he headed off for the livery.

Joe spotted Willy coming over the small rise and whispered, "Here he comes." Aymond picked up his saddle and headed to Jericho's stall. He waited until he could hear talking at the big double doors and then threw the saddle over Jericho. As Willy walked in he bent over to fasten the cinch. George was doing the same with Sparta. "Good morning. We're clearing out. Do we owe you anything else?"

"Nope, that's it." Willy turned back to the front doors and Ay led his horse out, followed by George.

Ay dropped the reins and grabbed Willy. "George, get his gun."

"What the hell!" exclaimed the surprised Willy. He struggled but Aymond held him steady. Brent and Joe rushed through door with pistols drawn.

George snatched his pistol while Joe growled, "We've got some serious questions for you Willy."

Aymond relaxed. It was a mistake. Willy pulled his gun arm lose and palming the derringer, shot at Joe, who slumped over. Willy turned to shoot at George but George had already leveled Willy's pistol and fired. The lead hit his wrist and the derringer's second shot went awry as George's second shot tore into Willy's stomach. He fell, twitching. George stepped back and lowered the hammer.

"Ya murdered my mother, ya belly crawlin' snake and now you'll die real slow. I'm glad ya tried for it."

"And what about Joe, George?" from Brent, who was kneeling beside Joe. George came up with a snap.

"Oh my God!"

Brent continued to check Joe who watched him with wide eyes. "You sure are one lucky bastard. Your buckle's holding the lead. It's just knocked the breath out of you. The worst you're goin' to have is a stomach ache, but that buckle will never keep your pants up again."

"I'll frame it and hang it on the wall," Joe gasped in a whisper.

"Good man," said Brent.

"But, I still feel miserable."

"It'll go quick. Now let's look at Willy." Willy's eyes were open and blood was pumping down his front. "Help me turn him, Ay. I need to check his back." They turned him partially on his side and Brent looked closer. "Like I thought. His spine's severed; he won't last long."

"Suffer you old bastard! Woman killin' son of a whore. You're goin' to rot in hell. Suffer, suffer!" George hissed through his teeth.

"Leave him be, George. You've got what you want. He knows retribution's at hand. Think of your own soul. Vengeance is mine saith the Lord. Let him be now," Aymond insisted.

"Oh, Ay, he's got it comin'. I may have been hasty with ma secon' shot but it was all movin' so fast. But he had every bit of it comin' an ya know that."

"I know, I know," Aymond agreed. "But you've got him and he knows it."

"I'm the boy you left tied to the wheel. You did in my Ma and then killed her and you've still got Blackie. I'm glad you're payin'."

Comprehension swept over Lindsey. "Oh, my back hurts. I've gottta git out of here and git ma gold." And the final realization overcame him that he was dying. The figure of George was becoming blurred. He screamed one time and died.

"Come on, George, He's gone and you got him. We'll need to do something about those kids. Brent, you'd better stay with Joe. Let the town people know the score. We don't need any new enemies. We'll check out Gertie."

George and Aymond rode up to the sod cabin where Gertie had a large tub on the fire and was scrubbing clothes. The kids were playing nearby. "Mrs. Gertrude Sharpe?" She nodded. "I'm Aymond Bearman and this is George Allen. Afraid I have some unpleasant news. Your husband's dead. He was a killer. Raped and killed George's mother and almost killed George. Excuse my bluntness but there's no other way to tell it."

"Thought it all along and he weren't my husband," she admitted. "Just kinda forced the kids and me to hang around. Wasn't much we could do." The little girl came running up and latched onto the side of Gertie's dress.

"What's these men doin' Gertie?"

"They came to tell us Willy's dead."

"Does that mean he won't hurt us no more?"

"Yeah."

"Ain't that good, Joey?"

Joey was watching intently. "How'd it happen?"

"He had killed this man's mother and when Willy pulled his gun he shot him," Aymond answered.

"Had it coming. He killed our mother and dad too. Nobody would believe us."

"Well, your ordeal's over now. We can see that you are sent back to your relatives. Who are your folks?"

"I don't want to leave Gertie. Don't let them take me Gertie," begged Sally.

"Yes, we'd rather stay with Gertie," said Joey. She's been good to us. She's not like Willy. We sure want to stay with Gertie. Ain't got no folks, anyway."

Gertie smiled and pulled the little girl to her as she ruffled Joey's hair.

"Well," Ay put in, "we can consider this settled. What do you think, George?"

"It's fine with me."

"How will you get along?"

"I'm strong, and I've got some savings tucked away." Gertrude smiled as she thought of the sack of gold. They would get by fine. "Don't worry about us, we'll make it," she said with assurance"

"Then it's settled," Ay smiled at Sally and she grinned back.

George and Aymond turned, mounted and rode toward the livery..

— — —

"Maybe we can run back over to Haley's Crossing and see the Matlocks," Ay suggested. "They'll want to know what happened. I bet Tucker and John really opened their eyes when they told them about the woman killed in that cabin northwest of the Crossing. Would have liked to have seen the look on their faces when Tucker told 'em they were suspected of that murder."

"Probably like to see them two gals too," guessed George.

"Reading my mind, are you? Well, say it right. It's those two girls, not them two gals."

Ay. I talks fine."

"You don't talk fine, but I'll let Molly work on you. She does it better."

"Yeah, and you're changin' the subject. I could tell you like them two."

"Those two,"

"Alright, Ay. Those two. But ya sho liked them."

"And we'll go see them too. Might take Cliff, if he's up to it, which I doubt. Yes, indeed, we'll see Miss Jenny and Miss Mary."

SUNSTONE PRESS

Send for our **free catalog**
and find out more about our books on:

- ❖ The Old West
- ❖ American Indian subjects
- ❖ Western Fiction
- ❖ Architecture
- ❖ Hispanic interest subjects
- ❖ And our line of full-color notecards

Just mail this card or call us on our toll-free number below

_____

Name

_____

Address

_____

City   State   Zip

Send Book Catalog _____ Send Notecard Catalog _____

Sunstone Press / P.O.Box 2321 / Santa Fe, NM 87504
(505) 988-4418   FAX (505) 988-1025   (800)-243-5644